Palm Trees in the Pyrenees

Palm Trees in the Pyrenees

Elly Grant

Books by the Author

Death in the Pyrenees series:

- Palm Trees in the Pyrenees
- Grass Grows in the Pyrenees
- Red Light in the Pyrenees
- Dead End in the Pyrenees
- Deadly Degrees in the Pyrenees

Angela Murphy series:

- The Unravelling of Thomas Malone
- The Coming of the Lord

Also by Elly Grant

- Never Ever Leave Me
- Death at Presley Park
- But Billy Can't Fly
- Twists and Turns

Chapter 1

His death occurred quickly and almost silently. It took only seconds of tumbling and clawing at air before the inevitable thud as he hit the ground. He landed in the space in front of the bedroom window of the basement apartment. As no one was home at the time and as the flat was actually below ground level, he may have gone unnoticed but for the insistent yapping of the scrawny, aged poodle belonging to the equally scrawny and aged Madame Laurent.

Indeed, everything in the town continued as normal for a few moments. The husbands who'd been sent to collect the baguettes for breakfast had stopped, as usual, at the bar to enjoy a customary glass of pastis and a chat with the patron and other customers. Women gathered in the little square beside the river, where the daily produce market took place, to haggle for fruit, vegetables and honey before moving the queue to the boucherie to choose the meat for their evening meals.

Yes, that day began like any other. It was a cold, crisp, February morning and the sky was a bright, clear blue just as it had been every morning since the start of the year. The yellow Mimosa shone out luminously in the morning sunshine from the dark green of the Pyrenees.

Gradually, word filtered out of the boucherie and down the line of waiting women that the first spring lamb of the season had made its way onto the butcher's counter, and everyone wanted some. Conversation switched from whether Madame Portes actually grew the Brussels sprouts she sold on her stall or simply bought them at the supermarket in Perpignan then resold them at a higher price, to speculating whether or not there would be sufficient lamb to go round. A notable panic rippled down the queue at the very thought of there not being enough as none of the women wanted to disappoint her family. That would be unacceptable in this small Pyrenean spa town, as in this small town, like many others in the region, a woman's place as housewife and mother was esteemed and revered. Even though many held jobs outside the home, their responsibility to their family was paramount.

Yes, everyone followed their usual routine until the siren blared out — twice. The siren was a wartime relic that had never been decommissioned even though the war had ended over half a century before. It was retained as a means of summoning the pompiers, who were not only the local firemen but also paramedics. One blast of the siren was used when there was a minor road accident or if someone took unwell at the spa but two blasts was for something extremely serious.

The last time there were two blasts was when a very drunken Jean-Claude accidentally shot Monsieur Reynard while mistaking him for a boar. Fortunately Monsieur Reynard recovered, but he still had a piece of shot lodged in his head which caused his eye to squint when he was tired. This served as a constant reminder to Jean-Claude of what he'd done as he had to see Monsieur Reynard every day in the cherry orchard where they both worked.

On hearing two blasts of the siren, everyone stopped in their tracks and everything seemed to stand still. A hush fell over the town as people strained to listen for the shrill sounds of the approaching emergency vehicles. Some craned their necks skyward hoping to see the police helicopter arrive from Perpignan and, whilst all were shocked that something serious had occurred, they were also thrilled by the prospect of exciting, breaking news. Gradually, the chattering restarted. Shopping was forgotten and the market abandoned. The boucherie was left unattended as its patron followed the crowd of women making their way to the main street. In the bar, the glasses of pastis were hastily swallowed instead of being leisurely sipped as everyone rushed to see what had happened.

As well as police and pompiers, a large and rather confused group of onlookers arrived outside an apartment building owned by an English couple called Carter. They arrived on foot and on bicycles. They brought ageing relatives, pre-school children, prams and shopping. Some even brought their dogs. Everyone peered and stared and chatted to each other. It was like a party without the balloons or streamers.

There was a buzz of nervous excitement as the police from the neighbouring larger town began to cordon off the area around the apartment block with tape. Monsieur Brune was told in no uncertain terms to restrain his dog, as it kept running over to where the body lay and was contaminating the area in more ways than one.

A slim woman wearing a crumpled linen dress was sitting on a chair in the paved garden of the apartment block, just inside the police line. Her elbows rested on her knees and she held her head in her hands. Her limp, brown hair hung over her face. Every so often she lifted her chin, opened her eyes and took in great, gasping breaths of air as if she was in danger of suffocating. Her whole body shook. Madame Carter, Belinda, hadn't actually fainted but she was close to it. Her skin was clammy and her pallor grey. Her eyes threatened at any moment to roll back in their sockets and blot out the horror of what she'd just seen.

She was being supported by her husband, David, who was visibly shocked. His tall frame sagged as if his thin legs could no longer support his weight and he kept swiping away tears from his face with the backs of his hands. He looked dazed and, from time to time, he covered his mouth with his hand as if trying to hold in his emotions but he was completely overcome.

The noise from the crowd became louder and more excitable and words like "accident," "suicide" and even "murder" abounded. Claudette, the owner of the bar that stood across the street from the incident, supplied the chair on which Belinda now sat. She realized that she was in a very privileged position, being inside the police line, so Claudette stayed close to the chair and Belinda. She patted the back of Belinda's hand distractedly, while endeavouring to overhear tasty morsels of conversation to pass on to her rapt audience. The day was turning into a circus and everyone wanted to be part of the show.

Finally, a specialist team arrived. There were detectives, uniformed officers, secretaries, people who dealt with forensics and even a dog handler. The tiny police office was not big enough to hold them all so they commandeered a room at the Mairie, which is our town hall.

It took the detectives three days to take statements and talk to the people who were present in the building when the man, named Steven Gold, fell. Three days of eating in local restaurants and drinking in the bars much to the delight of the proprietors. I presumed these privileged few had expense accounts, a facility we local police did not enjoy. I assumed that my hard earned taxes paid for these expense accounts yet none of my so called colleagues asked me to join them.

They were constantly being accosted by members of the public and pumped for information. Indeed everyone in the town wanted to be their friend and be a party to a secret they could pass on to someone else. There was a buzz of excitement about the place that I hadn't experienced for a very long time. People who hadn't attended church for years suddenly wanted to speak to the priest. The doctor who'd attended the corpse had a full appointment book. And everyone wanted to buy me a drink so they could ask me questions. I thought it would never end. But it did. As quickly as it had started, everybody packed up, and then they were gone.

Chapter 2

You must be wondering who is telling you this. Where are my manners? Allow me to introduce myself. My name is Danielle and I am a cop, or flic as I am called here in France. I hope you will be patient with me as English is not my first language.

I am attending the funeral of Steven Gold, the unfortunate man who fell from the apartment block owned by the Carters. He was a local businessman, and before he settled here in France, it is rumoured he'd been struck off as a solicitor in England. Most of the townspeople are here as all are curious. We don't get incidents like this happening very often, or indeed ever before, so it has caused a great deal of excitement and speculation. The gathering can be divided into the handful of people who liked the man, those who disliked or even hated him, rather more of them, in fact too many to count, and of course the usual group of religious or lonely people who attend every funeral.

Actually, most of the people attending disliked the man so much they're being guarded with their conversations lest someone thinks their negativity or ill feelings towards him may in some way have contributed to his death.

I was the first person on the scene that day as I was about to ticket an illegally parked car which was blocking an entrance outside the Carter's apartment block. People are always upset when they receive a parking ticket. They argue that they've only been gone for a minute or two or that their business was so urgent the law should bend for them. They are always unreasonable and usually blame me personally for their mistake.

On that day, I was at first more surprised than shocked when I saw him lying there. He had landed in an almost perfect foetal position and he fitted exactly into the small space outside the basement, bedroom window. His head was resting on a flowerpot and he looked comfortable. If it were not for the blood, one would have assumed he'd simply lain down when drunk and fallen asleep.

I had to call out to Madame Laurent and ask her to stand back and not come any closer as she was edging forward to see what had happened. Her yapping dog was making me nervous and I had enough to contend with without her having hysterics or a heart attack. One corpse was quite enough.

With jelly legs and shaking hands I went through the ritual of checking for a pulse, being careful not to touch anything except his wrist. I would have felt his neck where the pulse is easier to detect but I didn't want to get his blood on my hands. My heart was thumping and my fingers were sweating so much that I couldn't feel a thing, but it didn't matter, I knew he was dead. It would have been obvious to anyone.

His head was split almost in two and there was a lake of rapidly congealing blood under him. I was simply going through the motions as I'd been trained to do. I knew I'd be expected to write a report and, being a cop who dealt mostly with traffic offences or the occasional drunk, and being the only officer actually stationed in town, I didn't know what else to do as I'd had little experience of death. I hoped and prayed someone with more authority would arrive soon as a crowd was gathering and I was scared of losing control of the situation.

Chapter 3

The funeral service is relatively short and conducted both in French and English for the benefit of Steven's family and acquaintances from England. He'd been recently married for the second time and, in fact, some of the congregation had attended his wedding in this same small church only eight months before.

There is much unkind speculation that his Hungarian widow will miss him less than one might have expected because she now has his substantial fortune to keep her company and she no longer needs his permission to spend it. In this small town, people like to gossip and their words are rarely kind. Many people think that the young Hungarian man by the widow's side isn't really her cousin but actually her lover.

The gathering, as is the custom, has now moved to the town hall where food and wine have been laid on for the mourners. Few are mourning but all are partaking of the food and wine. As I look around me I see that dotted amongst the crowd are all the people who were present at the apartment block when Steven met his untimely death. All of them are foreigners, not one Frenchman amongst them. There are the Carters, of course, Belinda and David, and beside them stand their tenants Kurt and Rosa. Near the door is Byron who was a business associate of the deceased—he is accompanied by his son-in-law Mark—and just entering the hall is an English couple that I've seen once or twice in town but to whom I have yet to be formally introduced.

I don't consider myself to be racist but I'm not surprised that the apartment block is owned and frequented by foreigners. When the Carters first bought the building, they didn't carry out any repairs because they were contemptuous of their tenants and thought the shoddy standards were good enough for them. Now that the building requires essential work to be carried out, they don't have the money to pay for it.

Many of their tenants are lazy dropouts who say they are musicians, artists or actors. They come here expecting the fame that has previously eluded them but instead they end up living hand to mouth or on benefits. My hard work pays for their benefits and I resent it. Local people don't wish to be associated with these layabouts and they won't rent to them, even though the rent money comes directly from the government. But for Belinda and David Carter these tenants are a lifeline. The Carters have serious money worries and I have heard that the benefit money they receive each month in rent is all that stands between them and bankruptcy.

Many foreigners come here thinking they'll get rich quick. They assume that the local people, who've been running businesses for generations, are stupid. These incomers think they are smarter than us and therefore more able to 'cash in' as they say. They are like the palm trees that grow in this town in the Pyrenees, incongruous and out of place but here nevertheless.

If I sound bitter it is because I am. I resent these know-it-alls who look down on me and my neighbours. It's true of course that we locals often tolerate the incomers, and sometimes we even pretend to be their friends, but that's because we see them as easy pickings. It's always easy to part a fool from his money, particularly a greedy fool. Claudette, a local bar owner and occasional caterer, is the perfect example of good business sense. She has supplied the food and wine for this funeral at double the normal cost and the grieving widow cannot stop thanking her.

As I look around the room, I see Belinda Carter beckoning to me, trying to catch my attention. Dressed all in black from her feathered hat to her patent leather shoes, which are a remnant from her more prosperous days, she looks like a wounded crow. Her rail thin body stands slightly askew as she hugs her handbag to her chest. It seems as if one good gust of wind would carry her off up the mountain to be lost forever in the trees. Her gaunt expression and her facial twitches tell me she is barely hanging on to her composure.

"Bonjour, Belinda, ca va?" I say as I approach her. I feel I must be respectful.

She shrugs and her head shakes slightly but she does not return the pleasantry. Her lip trembles and I think that at any moment she will cry.

"Danielle, I must speak to you," she finally manages to say. Her eyes dart nervously about the room. "But not here," she adds dramatically. "Will you meet me tomorrow at my home after the children leave for school? My husband will be taking our friend to the airport at 10 o'clock so the house will be empty. I don't want to come to your office or everyone will know I've been speaking to you and you know how people like to gossip."

I stare into her eyes. She is pleading with me. She seems afraid, almost desperate.

"Is something wrong, Belinda? Is it anything to do with the death of Monsieur Gold?" I ask.

She nods slowly and her eyes fill with tears. "Yes," she says, almost in a whisper. "Please, Danielle, please come."

I look again at her tired face, she looks beaten and exhausted. She never fails to be polite to me but usually there is something in her eyes mocking me, but not today it seems. Today I see only despair.

Living in this town as an unmarried woman in my thirties and also a cop, I am left wide open to speculation about my sexuality. My boyish haircut and muscular physique, which I have achieved by visiting the gym three times a week, together with my authoritative manner, all contribute to me portraying a rather masculine appearance. The uniform doesn't help either as it's designed to be practical, not to show off curves. However, my not having a boyfriend or, indeed, wanting one doesn't mean I would prefer to date women.

I'm often hurt by the way I'm treated. I hear people whispering, calling me a lesbian flic or Monsieur Daniel. I'm not deaf and their comments cut me. For some reason they think it's acceptable to make sexist jokes at my expense, but it is not and I'm even more upset by the lack of respect I receive for the job I do. They simply don't understand that women can be police officers and do their job as well as any man.

Sometimes Belinda and her friends stop talking and stare at me when I enter a room. They snigger behind their hands or gossip with their heads held close together conspiratorially. Perhaps I'm being oversensitive. Perhaps it's simply because I'm a cop but I can't be certain. Now this woman wants my attention and maybe even my help. Tomorrow should be my day off but I'm curious to know what she has to say. Although I dislike her and therefore hesitate before answering, I hesitate for only a moment.

"Okay, Belinda, I will call on you. I'll come round at the time you suggest. Until tomorrow then."

She exhales audibly and her expression is one of relief.

"Thank you, Danielle," she says. "Thank you so much."

I give her a polite nod and say, "Au revoir, Belinda, a bientot."

She returns the gesture and I turn to walk away.

"After 10 o'clock, Danielle," she calls after me. "Remember, not before 10.00."

"Yes, after 10.00," I confirm. As I glance back at her, I see that she looks like a crumpled paper bag; all the stuffing is knocked out of her. The effort of speaking to me has drained her of all her reserves

Chapter 4

I make my way across the room to where the trestle tables laden with food and drinks are positioned. Steven's widow is standing beside one of the tables. She stands out from the crowd, dressed as she is in Chanel. I don't know much about fashion but everyone recognises the designers. There is something about a Chanel suit that makes it appropriate for every occasion. It must have cost a fortune and it looks to me as if she's already spending her inheritance. Everything about her screams money, from her perfectly coiffed hair to her cripplingly high stiletto heels. She is stylishly thin and I cannot help but be reminded of the saying that a woman can't be too rich or too thin. There is definitely something of the Wallis Simpson about this woman.

She's sipping red wine from a large glass and her head is cocked towards her 'cousin' who is standing facing her. He is tall and lean and he's dressed in a beautifully tailored suit; his shirt is white and crisply ironed. His high cheekbones and finely chiselled features are very handsome and make him stand out from this gathering. Most of the local people are short of stature and they dress simply, so a man such as this is easily noticed. He leans forward and speaks softly in the widow's ear and from time to time she touches his arm and smiles at him. To all who observe her, she seems an unlikely grieving widow.

"May I pour you some wine, Officer? You're not on duty are you?"

The voice startles me and I turn to see a slim, slightly built man proffering a bottle and a glass. He smiles at me and his face reminds me of a snake, with taut skin, thin lips and narrow eyes. His pupils are like cold, steel pinheads. His bald head accentuates this look. It is Kurt.

This Dutchman unnerves me like no other person can. There is something sly and dangerous about him. He smiles with his mouth but not with his eyes, in the same way that SS officers are depicted in films. I've known Kurt for four years having first met him at the Mairie when he arrived from Holland. He is another foreign, benefit parasite and he has a serious alcohol problem. Though he passes me in the street most days, this is the first time he has engaged me in conversation.

"Thank you, Kurt," I reply. "I'm not on duty at the moment so I will have a glass please."

He places the empty wine glass in my hand and fills it almost to the top with red wine. I prefer there to be some space in the glass to make it easier to hold and to allow the wine to breathe for a moment or two. But instead, I find myself having to sip it immediately to take the level down and make it less likely to spill.

"Did he jump or was he pushed, ha, ha?" he laughs.

What a strange thing to say, I think, particularly as we are at the man's funeral.

"I'm assuming you are talking about Steven Gold," I reply coldly then continue. "I guess that's something for the detective leading the investigation to find out. Why do you think he may have been pushed?"

"No particular reason," he says, still grinning menacingly. "Just making small talk."

I say nothing else but stand and sip my wine expecting him to move away, but he does not.

"Perhaps we should talk," he says.

"About anything in particular or do you just like my company?" I reply cheekily.

He scowls at me before continuing, "I just might have some information of interest to you."

"Information about what?" I ask. "I believe you were in the apartment block at the time of the man's death. Do you know something about the incident?"

"Perhaps indirectly," he says slowly. "I know some things about Rosa that might be important," he continues.

"Rosa?" I question "What has Rosa got to do with this?"

"I'll tell you," he replies, "but not here and not now. Perhaps we can meet in the café at Corsavy tomorrow. Tuesday's your day off isn't it? The day that all criminals are safe," he mocks. He leans forward and whispers in my ear, "Maybe you could buy me breakfast and I'll tell you what I know," he offers.

Having just made the arrangement to see Belinda, I won't be having a day off this week, but I've no wish to correct him. He makes my skin crawl. I consider what he's said for a moment and I'm intrigued. Why would he want to discuss Rosa? She's his girlfriend after all and they seem very close. I'm curious to hear what he has to say but I'm nervous about meeting him. Do I really want to be seen alone with this horrible man?

Finally, I decide that I'm more curious than repelled by him and I say, "I will meet you tomorrow, but you can buy me breakfast as it is you who wishes to speak to me. We can get together at 9 o'clock."

"Very well, Madame," he says, smirking. "You drive a hard bargain, until tomorrow then."

With that he clicks his heels, gives a small bow then turns and walks across the room to join Rosa. I wonder what that was all about, I think. How strange, how very, very strange.

Chapter 5

As I look around the room I see many familiar faces. This is a prestigious funeral and nobody wants to miss it. All the local dignitaries are here including the Mayor and his wife and the whole of the Commune Committee.

There is a photographer and a journalist from the local paper and even a journalist from one of the regional publications. Many people shake the widow's hand while smiling at the photographer. They all hope to be the one caught on camera with her and featured in the newspaper. This is the biggest event of the year and everyone wants their chance of fame.

Most people are standing in groups, divided by class and social standing, as is the custom. I notice the funeral director speaking to the chief clerk of the tax office and I can't help thinking that death and taxes are often linked.

As I observe the gathering, I see David Carter talking to the couple who are new in town. I would like him to introduce me to them, so I make my way over to where they're standing. All I know about them is that they're English and they arrived here six weeks ago intending to take up permanent residence. For some reason they were at the apartment block when Steven fell.

I know I must make a point of speaking to David as he has caused many problems over parking. Once again, I'll have to explain to him that he cannot mark out parking spaces in front of his apartment block and then rent them to his tenants. The street is a public thoroughfare and is owned by everyone equally so he must not deface it or block it with traffic cones. I've had several complaints regarding his cavalier attitude and I must now tackle the problem. At first I thought he was simply being stupid and perhaps this sort of behaviour was acceptable in England, but now I believe he is arrogant and I'm annoyed. Maybe he thinks he can make a fool out of me but he's wrong, very wrong.

"David," I say as I tap him on the arm. He swings round and there is a look of mock surprise on his face.

"Oh, hello, Danielle," he replies.

He looks like an overgrown schoolboy. He has a youthful face that is quite handsome. His fringe flops on his forehead and he flicks it away, then he adopts an expression which is reminiscent of the actor Hugh Grant who I'm sure he's trying to emulate. Many women find him attractive and he has impeccable manners, but I find him irritating. He's weak and he is, as the English say, a clown. He's obviously not going to introduce me to the couple in his company, but it is of no matter as the gentleman introduces himself.

"Bonjour," he begins. "Je m'appelle Alan. Je me presente ma femme Charlotte." He holds his upturned hands in front of his wife as if he is presenting me with a plate of food.

His wife is a slim woman with straight blonde hair and serious blue eyes. She holds out her hand to shake mine. Her handshake is soft and her thin hand slides through mine barely touching it. Her clothes are clean and smart but mismatched and a bit young for her. Alan looks rather dishevelled. His hair is long and straggly and his cheeks are stubbly. His clothes are untidy and seem to be wearing him instead of the other way round. Both Alan and Charlotte are dressed in rather brightly coloured attire for a funeral, I observe.

I turn to Alan. "You speak French," I say. "Tres bien, Monsieur."

"Not very much and not very well," he replies with a shy smile. "I've had only five lessons."

"Well that's five more than I've had," David says with a smirk. "And I've been here for four years."

"Perhaps that's why you have difficulty making French friends," I say, unable to stop myself. "After all, Monsieur, it is you who is the foreigner in this town."

He looks slightly embarrassed and he gives a shrug. "My children speak French," he says. "And Belinda is fluent." As if somehow their abilities compensate for his lack of language skills. "I've just been too busy to learn," he continues. "You know how it is."

Yes, I think, I do know how it is. You are too busy sitting at home playing computer games or surfing the internet or perhaps you are too busy drinking in the bar every evening and being the last one to leave.

The truth is he is lazy. Before he moved his family here, he had a good job in London. He didn't have to work too hard and he didn't have to be too smart, he simply had to commute for an hour each day, shuffle some papers then pick up his cheque at the end of the month. He couldn't contemplate failure and he thought living in France would be an easier life. A 'doddle' is what he said. I am astounded that this stupid man uprooted his family and sold everything they owned and is now attempting to run a business he has no experience of, in a country where he has no knowledge of the language or the customs. My previous description of him was correct. He is indeed, a clown.

"Did you know Steven Gold, the man who was killed?" I ask Alan and Charlotte.

"We met him very briefly when we tried to purchase an apartment he was selling but unfortunately, through circumstances beyond our control, the deal fell apart," Charlotte replies. "David was coming to the funeral and he suggested we accompany him so he could introduce us to some people. You might think this an odd place to socialise but we see a funeral as a celebration of life and therefore a happy event rather than a sad one."

I don't really understand their way of thinking but they seem to be inoffensive, gentle people, so I don't judge them.

"I'm intending to come to your office later today," David says, "perhaps at about three o'clock. There's something I want to discuss with you about this unfortunate business. It concerns Mark."

"Mark?" cuts in Charlotte. "Our Mark, who we were buying the apartment from?"

"Yes, that's right," continues David. "But its all right, it has nothing to do with either of you," he adds hastily.

"And I would like to speak to you, David," I reply, "about the parking."

He hangs his head in mock shame.

"Ah, the parking," he says, "the bane of my life."

I turn to Alan and Charlotte and ask them, "Would it be possible for you both to come to my office after this gathering is over? I've noticed that whilst I do have your statements regarding this unfortunate event, they're not signed. It's just a formality, nothing to worry about. It's simply because you were in the building when the man fell to his death," I add.

"Mais oui," says Alan, smiling. "Of course, it's not a problem."

I cannot help but like this man. He looks like a hippy with his long hair and untidy clothes but he seems gentle and shy and he is trying so very hard to please.

"Till later then, Messieurs, Madame," I say.

They each acknowledge with a nod and Alan smiles his goofy smile.

"Enchante," he says.

Chapter 6

I always find funerals tiring as everyone feels they must participate in small talk and this gathering is no different. I haven't paid my respects to the widow yet as she is constantly surrounded by people who wish to be acquainted with her. Neither have I had time to speak to my friend Patricia who works for the funeral director as she's been busy behind the scenes.

However, it occurs to me that I have somehow become very popular. Indeed my attention has been sought by three of the seven people who were present in the building at the time of Steven's untimely death. Before today, I've shared only passing pleasantries with them as we've passed each other in the street. Now, they call me by my first name and treat me as if I were a close acquaintance.

As I glance around the room, I see a gentleman kissing the hand of the merry widow. Her 'cousin' is not amused and his face is like thunder. It makes me chuckle. The gentleman isn't a young man but he is handsome and charming. His lean, elegant frame is clothed by Armani and he wears it well. He's polished, from his black hat which he wears cocked slightly over one eye, to his black patent leather shoes. It is Byron. He's the archetypal English gentleman and he makes me think of James Bond. If we meet, he's always kind to me. He calls me 'Mademoiselle' but manages to say this in a respectful way that doesn't undermine my authority.

"I see the old dog is up to his usual tricks."

A tall young man with flaming red hair sidles up to me. It's Mark, Byron's son-in-law. He winks at me and looks pointedly at Byron.

"Vol-au-vent?" he asks holding a plate towards me. "I see you've met the new folk," he continues, cocking his head towards Alan and Charlotte.

"Yes," I reply. Then add, "I was very sorry to hear that your apartment sale has fallen through. I know how much work you put into the renovation."

"Yeah, sods law," he replies. "Just when everything seemed so solid, it all fell apart."

"Alan and Charlotte seem nice people. They must be disappointed too. It's a real shame," I say.

"Yeah, yeah," he replies. "But sometimes all is not as it seems. I could have really done with the money what with the baby and all. The way the economy is at the moment, I just don't know how long it'll be before I find another buyer."

I'm sorry that Mark is looking so deflated. He's usually upbeat and cheerful and one rarely sees him without a smile on his face. He's rather a striking figure in this town with his tall, strong physique and flaming red hair. His bright eyes are a piercing green and his expression is always gentle. In this spa town, where many people are middle-aged or elderly, he really stands out from the crowd.

His wife is equally striking. She is tall and willowy with a classically beautiful face. It's easy to tell that she's Byron's daughter as even her mannerisms are similar to his. Their child looks like a plump little cherub. He has inherited his mother's sweet mouth and his father's vivid green eyes and flaming red hair. When they are in the street many local ladies approach them to coo over the baby or stroke his round, little cheeks. They approve of this family and want them to remain here as they bring new blood to this old town. They respect the fact that both Mark and his wife Elizabeth speak perfect French and many people call them 'friend.' Indeed, they are no longer seen as tourists, they're now treated as of the town. Perhaps their son's children, should they remain here, will eventually be treated as locals.

"Actually, Danielle, I'd like to have a word with you about Alan and Charlotte. There's something about them that worries me," Mark says. "They told me some things I think you ought to know. It's probably nothing, but if I tell you, then you can decide and my conscience will be clear."

"Do you want to talk now?" I ask glancing at my watch. "I could give you half an hour. Is that enough time?"

"Sorry, Danielle," he says. "But I'm due at the notaire's office in twenty minutes to get some advice on this whole sorry mess. I don't know if anything can be done. I doubt it but I have to investigate every possibility because I need the money."

I am genuinely sorry for the young man but the truth is everyone knew that the apartment was grossly overpriced. In fact, I heard that Steven was rubbing his hands with glee at the prospect of the fat commission cheque he would receive for creating the sale. Everyone knew it was far too expensive. Everyone, that is, except Alan and Charlotte.

"How about tomorrow?" he suggests.

I'm seeing Kurt for breakfast and Belinda after that, but at this time of the year, with the spa having just reopened after the winter break, there is virtually no work for me to do and besides it would normally have been my day off.

"I can see you in the afternoon," I offer. "How about three o'clock."

"Yeah, yeah that will be good," he replies. "I'll see you then. I'd better go and rescue the widow and her boyfriend from that old devil." He stares pointedly in Byron's direction. "The boyfriend looks like he might have a stroke if Byron lingers there much longer."

We both laugh and exchange knowing looks and he heads off across the room towards his father-in-law.

Chapter 7

I'm beginning to wonder if one of these people, so anxious to speak to me, may in fact have seen something significant about Steven's fall. I wrack my brains to try to remember where everyone was in the building at the time, but it's no use. Everything happened in a blur and all I can remember is the blood. However, I reason, if they had seen something important they would surely have advised the investigating officer, if only to excuse themselves as a possible suspect in a crime. I've seen all their statements as I've been allocated the important job of filing them. The only job a female cop is deemed capable of, it seems, but there was nothing significant in them.

The room is beginning to empty as Byron makes his way towards me. "Bonjour, Mademoiselle," he says, bowing deeply and kissing my hand. "And how is my favourite officer of the law?" he asks. "I must say you look particularly charming today. It's nice to see you out of that sack of a uniform."

I find myself blushing as I'm not used to compliments.

"Oh, I am sorry, my dear," he continues. "I didn't mean to embarrass you."

"I saw you talking to the widow and her cousin," I say, trying to change the subject from myself. "What are they like? I believe they are Hungarian and there is speculation that she may have links to royalty."

"Royalty my eye!" he exclaims with a laugh. "She is certainly from Eastern Europe but don't let the fancy clothes fool you. Steven met her on an internet dating site and created that story to make her sound less sordid. They were married three months after they met. Look at her, Danielle. She's half his age. It was all about a lonely old sod who wanted sex and a greedy young woman prepared to do anything for money and opportunity."

"But I heard there was some sort of pre-nuptial agreement," I say. "Surely she'll get nothing."

"Yes, my dear, there was, but it covered only divorce, not death, so it looks as if she'll get the lot."

"But didn't he have a daughter in England?"

"You are absolutely right. He has a daughter and she does live in England but they hadn't spoken to each other in over two years. He also has an English will but he didn't make a will here in France when he married. The way things are conducted under French law, I believe that means Magda, his widow, and Carol, his daughter, will each get half of everything. And as most of Steven's fortune is here in France, the widow will get a substantial sum."

"Considering they were together for such a short time she must be feeling very fortunate to have married such a wealthy man," I observe.

"I have heard that his daughter is going to challenge the will through the court but it could take years and in the meantime Magda can withdraw everything that's in the joint account which, if I've heard correctly, contains over two million Euros. Then, of course, there's the private estate they called home. It's worth another couple of million and it was bought in joint names so the most that Magda could lose is twenty five percent. I'm sure there is much more squirreled away that neither Carol nor the court will ever know about."

"I knew he was well off but I had no idea he was so very wealthy," I say.

"You don't know the half of it, Danielle. Steven made money out of everyone."

There is a bitter edge to his voice. I know Byron had some business dealings with Steven but I don't know what was involved.

"Would you look at that pathetic creature," he says, changing the subject and with a nod in Belinda's direction. "What a state she's in."

"She's been like that since Steven's fall," I reply. "She seems very shocked and very depressed. It's as if she's shrunk and aged and become lifeless and dull. She was so vivacious when they first moved here from England."

"Perhaps she has a guilty conscience," he says with a wry smile.

"Do you know something, Monsieur, that I do not?" I ask.

"Maybe yes, maybe no," he replies mysteriously. He pauses for a moment as if deep in thought then looks me directly in the eye and asks, "Would you do me the honour of dining with me tonight, Danielle? It will give me the opportunity to tell you what I know and it would do my reputation no harm to be seen with a younger woman."

He smiles his charming smile and his twinkling eyes make me blush once again. I'd love to have dinner with this attractive man if I can just muster up the courage. I know I'd be safe with him, as it wouldn't be a date as such and, besides, he's always respectful.

"It's very kind of you to ask me, Byron. I would love to accept your kind invitation."

"Good, I'll pick you up at 7.00. Give me your address," he says. "I know a fantastic restaurant in Maurellies. It serves the best wild boar I've ever tasted and the chef bought top quality truffles from the truffle fair last week, so we'll be in for a real treat. The place is rather exclusive, few local people know about it as it's out of town. It will afford us privacy when we speak."

I quickly scribble down my address and hand it to him. I am both happy and disappointed at the remoteness of the venue he's suggested. Part of me would like local people to see me dining with Byron as it would be considered quite a status symbol but the other part would feel embarrassed and uncomfortable. However, he obviously doesn't wish our conversation to be overheard and the restaurant sounds superb.

"Till seven then, lovely lady." he says and once again he bows and kisses my hand.

"Till seven," I agree.

"Now, if you will excuse me, I think I'll go back and annoy the 'cousin' for a bit more sport," he says with a devilish smile and a wink of his eye. With that, he turns and walks away.

True to his word, I watch Byron as he goes over to the widow and this time he casually drapes his arm around her waist. Her cousin storms off to the drinks table, fills his glass with wine and gulps it down. It does indeed seem that Byron has rattled his chains once again.

How curious it is, I think, that now another person wishes a private talk with me regarding Steven's death. I feel rather nervous about all these meetings. Whatever will they tell me I wonder?

Chapter 8

As there's hardly anyone left in the room, Claudette and her assistant are beginning to clear the tables. I see Rosa standing beside the window to the side of the room. She's talking to Father Francis, our local priest. I am not keen on Father Francis as he's a bit of a busy-body, rather judgemental and very old fashioned. I try to avoid him if I can as he's always telling me that marriage is a holy state and children are a blessing. He says this is the path that God intends for me. He's constantly suggesting single men he thinks I should meet and he always offers to speak to them on my behalf. I'm sure my mother is in cahoots with him and it's extremely embarrassing.

I'm delighted to see that Rosa is looking very well. She is recovering from glandular fever and her hair, which had become quite thin and straggly, has just grown back to its former glory. It's cut in a modern, short style which perfectly frames her pretty, elfin features. Her slender body and petite frame together with impeccable dress sense give her a very chic, French look. But Rosa is not from these parts; she is South African. It's only when you speak to her and she replies in her inimitable, animated way that you realise her fiery, vivacious manner could never be French. We French are much more reserved, much more sedate and consequently, much less colourful.

Rosa's expression is serious and her eyes are downcast. Father Francis is speaking to her and from time to time she looks up and nods; she's obviously concentrating on what he's saying. After a few minutes, the conversation ends and I see her heading towards Belinda who's sitting alone on a chair at the back of the room. I watch as Rosa approaches her and begins to speak. Then Rosa reaches out and places her arm protectively around her shoulders as Belinda begins to cry. Belinda's sobbing gets louder and everyone begins to mutter. It's not appropriate for her to be sobbing so loudly when the widow is not crying at all. Rosa looks slightly panic stricken, so I cross the room to offer my assistance.

"Ladies," I say. "May I help you?"

Rosa seems relieved. "Hello, Danielle, I'm so glad to see you," she replies.

Belinda looks up at me from her chair then cries even louder than before. She is moaning and wailing, her eyes are red and her cheeks are wet with tears. Her shoulders are heaving from the sobbing and every so often a hiccupping sound escapes from her throat.

"What's set her off?" I ask Rosa.

"I don't know," she replies. "All I said was that Kurt and I were very sorry about what had happened at her apartment and that Kurt asked me to send her his regards. He particularly asked me to tell Belinda that she was in his thoughts. I said nothing upsetting or hurtful. In fact, Kurt didn't come over himself because he's in dispute with David over the rent and he didn't want to involve Belinda when she's been so troubled."

With this, Belinda groans a long, "Oh nooo," and continues to sob loudly.

"I think we'd better get her out of here," I suggest. "She's making everyone feel uncomfortable."

"May I help?" Father Francis asks and I realise he's standing behind me. "Perhaps you would like me to pray with you?"

"I think we can manage, thank you, Father," I say coldly; prayers are the last thing I want to hear. "Belinda just needs some fresh air."

Father Francis stands back as Rosa and I grip Belinda under her arms and practically carry her from the room. I wonder why the kind words from Kurt have upset Belinda so much, but this isn't the time to ask her.

Rosa goes off to find David and I support Belinda as we stand on the pavement. She seems very fragile and her whole body is trembling. I'm frightened to grip her too strongly in case I bruise her. When Rosa and David return, Rosa and I manoeuvre Belinda into the car so David can drive her home. As the car pulls away, Rosa sighs with relief.

"I didn't know what to do there," she says. "Thanks for helping me."

"Don't mention it, Rosa, it's nothing," I reply. "How are you keeping? You look well."

"Thanks for your kind words, Danielle. I'm feeling good and Kurt has been looking after me very well."

I can't understand why someone as lovely as Rosa would be attracted to a ghastly man like Kurt. He's a drunk with no money and he's not even attractive. I don't like the man and I wonder if perhaps he'll betray Rosa's trust when I meet him for breakfast tomorrow.

"This whole affair about Steven has been horrible, hasn't it?" she continues. "Do you think he could have been murdered?" Her voice is low and secretive. "He wasn't liked, you know. I overheard David shouting at him on the morning he died. I live in one of the second floor apartments and they were directly above me; the noise woke me up."

"Did you tell the detective?" I ask.

"Pah, that chauvinist pig," she spits. "I didn't tell him anything, but I know something that I'll tell you, Danielle."

She glances around to make sure no one can overhear us then she looks towards the door to where Alan is standing. He waves to us.

"I can see the new couple are waiting for you just now. I'll pop round to your office on Wednesday as I've an appointment at the doctor tomorrow. I'll come at lunchtime and bring you some of my special chilli for your lunch," she offers.

I'm delighted as Rosa's chilli is legendary. I agree and arrange a time then I make my way over to Alan and Charlotte who are, indeed, waiting for me.

Chapter 9

As we make our way down the street towards my office, Alan says 'bonjour' to everyone we pass and, as is the custom, they return the greeting. Charlotte looks at him and smiles like an indulgent parent of a precocious child.

"Isn't this fantastic?" Alan exclaims. "The people here are so friendly. This wouldn't happen in England."

He is correct of course. In this town, people are friendly. In fact, nobody would dream of entering a shop without greeting all who were inside or leaving that shop without saying 'Monsieurdame' as they exit. The habit of running Monsieur and Madame together has become commonplace because of the amount of use the words get.

"So you think you'll stay here?" I ask, "Even with the apartment purchase falling through."

As soon as the words are out of my mouth, I regret saying them as Alan looks crestfallen.

"It's been such a disappointment," he replies. "Hasn't it, love?" he turns to Charlotte.

"Oh yes," she agrees. "We were gutted and it looks as if we'll lose our deposit even though none of it was our fault. But we do plan to stay on here, nevertheless. If we can find some work."

"Would it help to talk about it? Is there anything I can do? You shouldn't lose your deposit if you've done nothing wrong."

"That is so kind of you," Charlotte replies, and she stresses the word so. She smiles at me but I notice she hasn't actually taken me up on my offer.

We reach the end of the main street and cut through a small square that leads to the river. I see the florist has placed a lovely display of flowering plants on the street in front of his shop. I'm impressed that even in February he has achieved a display so colourful and beautiful.

We then pass the small local cinema which also serves as a theatre and I glance up at the advertising board to see what's on. As a single lady, it's acceptable for me to attend the theatre or cinema on my own and I look forward to every new movie or production.

We have almost reached my office which is actually not much more than a room and a toilet in a single story building. However, it does at least have one thing going for it as it has almost a whole wall of windows which overlook the river Tech and the mountains beyond. Most days are sunny. Indeed, we average over 320 days of sunshine each year, so my views are spectacular.

"Can we stop and look at the river?" asks Alan.

"Of course, Darling," Charlotte replies. "I'm sure we can spare a minute or two. I'm sure Danielle won't mind."

I am standing right beside her yet she hasn't actually asked me but I feel obliged to indulge Alan's request. It strikes me that their relationship is more like mother and son than that of husband and wife. It seems that Alan asks Charlotte's permission for everything he does and she always indulges him. What I perceived as charming is now making me feel rather uncomfortable as I'm being drawn into accepting what is obviously a common scenario for them but rather creepy to the outside observer.

We stand and look down at the river as it courses over the boulders which have been washed down from higher up the mountain. There hasn't been much rain and the river is quite low, but it's still fast flowing.

Alan marvels at how clear it is. "The water comes straight off the mountain tops when the snow melts," he explains to me, as if I am a tourist and he is my guide. "Would you look at those ducks," he continues, "Have you ever seen such fat ducks? That's because the river is full of fish."

I pointedly look at my watch. "I'm sorry," I say, "but we must move on now as I've work to do this afternoon."

"There swims dinner," says Alan, pointing to a duck and chuckling to himself. He has continued as if I haven't spoken.

Then Charlotte touches his arm and says, "Alan, Darling, we have to go now," and he follows her like an obedient puppy.

We enter the office and I offer them coffee which they accept. Then I excuse myself for a moment and quickly change back into my uniform in the toilet.

"I'll just get those statements," I say when I return.

Charlotte turns to me. "You know we heard something that isn't in our statements. It's probably nothing, but you never know. If you have the time, we can talk about it. We feel comfortable speaking to you. I didn't take to that investigating detective one little bit."

Here we go again, I think, as I unlock the filing cabinet to retrieve the paperwork.

Chapter 10

My hands shake slightly as I place the coffees on the desk, then I sit down on my leather swivel chair and take a notepad and pen from the drawer. I'm apprehensive about what they're about to tell me. If the information is useful, and it can help to prove that Steven's fall was an accident and not suicide or murder, it might help to bring the investigation to a swift end. Inspector Gerard is desperate to close this case as he's run out of things to investigate and nobody who was present in the building at the time has given him any significant information.

Charlotte glances at Alan and purses her lips. She looks serious and I'm worried she might be having second thoughts about talking to me. I decide not to press her for the information but instead I try to put them both at their ease by asking them about themselves.

"So," I begin. "How did you choose this town for your new life? Do you know someone who lives here?"

Charlotte visibly relaxes and says, "We wanted a fresh start. It's a second marriage for both of us and we're at the stage of our lives when our children are grown and we've a bit of money saved. We found it so claustrophobic living in a modern box of a house, on a boring council estate. When instead we could have the freedom to stay in a place like this and be surrounded by these beautiful mountains." She sweeps her hand towards the view out of the window.

"It's great here isn't it?" Alan adds. "We are so at one with nature. Did you know Charlotte's a healer? She understands it all, crystals, dowsing, colour therapy, and she can read Tarot cards. She's going to start her own business to help people here, because the 'curists' who come for treatments at the spa are already used to alternative therapies and they're open- minded."

"That's right," agrees Charlotte, "and Alan is a wonderful carpenter. He used to design sets for a theatre in England. We're sure his skills will be transferable and he'll be able to get work here."

"When we saw the ad on Steven's website for Mark's apartment, we sold our house and packed all our worldly goods into our van and headed across the Channel," Alan adds. "We knew even before we saw the apartment that it would be perfect for us."

"Yes," agrees Charlotte, smiling at Alan. "We just know these things. Don't we, Darling?"

How odd, I think, I cannot imagine anyone packing up their life and then travelling to a foreign country with all their worldly goods in a van, on a whim. The longer I am in the company of Alan and Charlotte the stranger they seem. Now they're more relaxed and have almost finished their coffees, I decide to try to extract the information about Steven.

"How about another coffee?" I offer, in as friendly a fashion as I can muster. "Then you can tell me what you overheard."

"That would be lovely," Charlotte says and gives me the same slow smile she uses for Alan.

Chapter 11

I place the fresh coffees on the table and notice that Charlotte is holding Alan's hand. "It's all right, Love," she says. "No need to be upset. He just gets a bit anxious sometimes," she explains to me. "This whole business is rather upsetting."

As I suspect that the information I'm about to be told might be rather lengthy, I abandon my notebook and pen and, instead, retrieve a rather old tape recorder from my desk drawer. "If you have no objection, I'll tape this conversation as my shorthand is very poor," I explain.

Alan looks at the old machine and chuckles. "That looks brand new and it's an ancient model," he says. "I bet it's hardly ever been used."

"It has never been used," I reply. "Fortunately it has a mains connection or we would be in trouble as I can't remember ever changing the batteries."

I plug it in, press the record button and the machine whirrs into action. Alan gives me a 'thumbs up' sign.

"I'm not sure where to begin," Charlotte says.

"Why don't you start by telling me why you were at the apartment block, where you were situated in the building, and then what you heard," I prompt.

"Very well," says Charlotte and she begins. "When the purchase fell through, we were living in the Hotel Paris and, as you must know, it's not cheap. We do have some money behind us but we're not rich so we don't want to waste any of it. I'd met David a few times in the cafe and told him about our predicament. He was very sympathetic. He said we weren't alone in having problems with one of Steven's deals and he told me that he had an apartment available for rent which might suit us. He said that by renting from him, instead of staying in a hotel, our costs would be cut significantly, and when I looked at the figures I agreed with him. So we arranged to meet him at the apartment on the day of the incident." She stops to sip her coffee and Alan begins to speak.

"You know the layout of the building, Danielle," he says. Then he explains, "There's the basement flat which is let to an elderly lady who was visiting her daughter that day and, adjacent to that, is the storage room. The ground floor has an apartment with three bedrooms and it's let to a family from Toulouse, but they were also away that day. Then there's the first floor. The right hand apartment has two bedrooms and is about to be rented to a single lady who's a foreign language teacher. We were looking at the left-hand apartment. It only has one bedroom but it has a huge balcony which extends over the roof of the adjacent boulangerie. Above that, on the second floor, are the apartments which are rented to Kurt and Rosa. Kurt has the two bedroom apartment and Rosa has the one bedroom apartment. Above that again, on the third floor, is the big apartment that Steven fell from. David told me the layout because he thought I might be able to help him with one or two repairs."

"So you were on the first floor and Steven was on the third floor," I confirm and they both nod.

"Then what happened?"

"Well, let me see," Charlotte continues. "We were standing on the balcony looking out over the street as it was a beautiful, warm, sunny day."

"Yes," confirms Alan. "We were marvelling that I was wearing a T-shirt in February. We couldn't do that in England, mais non," he says, "mais non, indeed."

"Steven was on the third floor balcony with Byron, and from the conversation we overheard, Byron was not a happy man," Charlotte says. "We hadn't been introduced to Byron at that time, but we now know who he is. So I can confirm he is the same man who we overheard then met in the grounds of the apartment block after Steven's fall." She continues, "Byron's voice was raised and he was accusing Steven of ripping him off for the money from some business deal. Steven was at first trying to pacify him. He kept saying to Byron that he didn't know why he was making such a fuss when he had an airtight contract written up by the notaire. Then Byron said that Buttonet, the notaire, was a crook and was in Steven's pocket and he didn't trust either of them not to steal his money." She pauses for a moment to sip her coffee and to catch her breath, then continues, "Steven said he was being ridiculous, and that the position of notaire was overseen by the government, and of course Monsieur Buttonet wasn't a crook." She turns to Alan. "That's right so far isn't it, Darling?"

"There or thereabouts," he says, nodding his head in agreement.

She continues, "Byron asked Steven where the money was? Why hadn't it been transferred to his business account? Then Steven said something like, 'You know how things are Byron, I've simply been too busy to do the paperwork but it'll get done this week. I promise you'll have your money by next week at the latest.' "

Alan cuts in, "Tell her about the death threat, Charlotte."

"Oh, yes," she continues. "Byron was very, very angry; we could feel the tension in the air even though we were two floors below them. His voice was raised and he said it had better be the case because if he fucked with him, so help him, he'd swing for him." She pauses, then says, "Please excuse my language, but they're his words not mine."

" 'Swing for him.' What does that mean?" I ask. "I've never heard that saying."

"It's a death threat," Alan says. "It suggests Byron would be prepared to hang for his actions. Do you understand, Danielle?"

"Ah, that explains it for me, thank you, Alan. I've never heard Byron swear, he is always a gentleman, so he must have been enraged by Steven."

"Then things became even more heated, didn't they Darling?" Charlotte says and Alan nods in agreement. "Steven's voice went very cold; he said to Byron, 'Just remember, little man, you're a small fish in a small pond and I am a barracuda. Don't think you can speak to me like that and don't think you can lecture me. If you try to mess with me, I'll chew you up and spit you out. You were nothing until you met me and you can be nothing again.'" She pauses for dramatic effect.

"And you are sure you heard all this clearly?" I ask.

"Oh yes, definitely. Perhaps I haven't repeated everything word perfectly but that's the gist of what was said," she says. "The street is so narrow at that point and there are buildings all around so sounds echo. We heard their conversation very clearly. Besides they were shouting so loudly, the conversation would've been hard to ignore."

I notice the coffees I've served are hardly touched and have gone cold. Charlotte is looking rather drained. "Shall I make some fresh, hot coffee?" I ask.

"Oh, yes please," they say in unison.

I quickly make the coffees and place a handful of biscuits on a plate in front of them, then I ask Charlotte to continue.

"It went quiet for a few minutes. When they resumed their conversation, they were talking about Byron buying an apartment block at a cut price then reselling it for a huge profit. Steven said that the current owners were nearly bankrupt and would accept just about anything to save themselves from going under."

"Then we heard Steven mention David and Belinda and we realised it was the block we were standing in that he was referring to," Alan adds.

"Byron asked why he should trust Steven when he was still waiting to be paid for the last deal. Steven said Byron should do what he was told or he'd find someone else to do the deal then Byron would get nothing. We felt he was inferring that Byron would get none of the money owed to him, never mind money from the newly proposed deal. Then it went quiet so we went inside as the conversation seemed to be over and we didn't want them to notice us eavesdropping."

"Where was David when this conversation was taking place? I thought he was with you."

"We were alone," Charlotte says. "David had been summoned to Rosa's flat because her heating had stopped working. David said it was probably the pilot light and he would go and restart it for her. He was gone rather a long time but we didn't mind because it let us get a feel of what the apartment was like. In fact, we didn't see David again until after Steven had fallen. We met him in the corridor when everyone was rushing outside."

"What made you leave the apartment?" I ask. "Did you see or hear anything?"

"All we heard was the little dog yapping," Alan replies.

"And some sort of disturbance in the corridor as people went to investigate," Charlotte adds.

"And that is everything you saw and heard?" I ask.

"Yes, absolutely," Charlotte confirms.

I stop the tape and stare at the paperwork on my desk. The statements they'd previously made consisted of a paragraph each, and said nothing, other than confirming they were present in the building at the time of Steven's fall.

"I'll have to consider the significance of what you've told me," I say. "I may have to call you back in to sign new statements. You've no need to be concerned as you've done nothing wrong. Indeed, your new statements serve to show me you were nowhere near Steven when he fell."

"So we can go now?" Alan asks and he stands up. He is nervous and twitchy and anxious to leave.

"Yes, of course," I reply.

As I show them to the door I say, "I take it you've not become one of David's tenants. How may I contact you?"

Charlotte advises me that they've rented an apartment from the patron of the café and she gives me the address together with the number of her mobile phone. Then they thank me for my time and leave. I watch them as they walk away from the office hand in hand like a pair of teenagers. Even with all that's happened they still seem to be in a different world from the rest of us.

Chapter 12

I listen to the tape and make notes on what they've told me. It occurs to me that, although Alan and Charlotte perceive the conversation they've overheard to be Byron making a serious threat towards Steven, this is unlikely to be the case. I don't think Byron would have done anything to harm him. Indeed, the timing of Steven's death could mean that Byron will have great difficulty in recovering his money in spite of his having a contract. This might explain the close attention he was paying to the widow at the funeral. It also confirms that Steven was unlikely to be suicidal. He obviously had it all: a new wife, plenty of money and, more importantly for him, power.

My head is buzzing and I need to get some fresh air. I check my watch and see I've over an hour until David is due to call on me, so I decide to lock up the office and head across the bridge towards the petanque courts. They are situated on the edge of the river bank and shaded by tall, plane trees. It's a very picturesque spot and there are benches to sit on. It should be quiet at this time of day as many people will be at home eating their mid-day meal.

As I arrive at the benches, I am greeted by a handful of the elderly men who live in the retirement apartments on this side of the river. They are here for the companionship and the petanque which is played every day except Sunday. They don't play on Sundays because that's the day families visit each other. Granddads play with grandchildren while daughters cook dinner. Most of these men have known me since

I was born and they think it's funny when they see me in my uniform. They don't consider me to be a real policewoman and treat me as if I am simply a traffic warden, because in their eyes, a real officer of the law will always be a man.

I sit down on a bench in the sunshine and stretch my legs out in front of me, crossing them at the ankles. I'm facing the river where fat ducks swim up and down. Every so often an excitable quacking, dipping, flapping of wings and feet over head occurs. It's relaxing to watch them and, like counting sheep leaping over fences, it makes my eyelids feel heavy, so I shut my eyes and let my head loll back. My ears are filled by a cacophony of birdsong and a gentle breeze blows around me and rustles the branches of the trees. I don't know when I fell asleep, or for how long I've slept, but I am rudely awakened by one of the elderly petanque players. He is shaking my arm and I awake with a start to see Bernard, who is a friend of my father, facing me. He's smiling, his plump face has white whiskers sprouting untidily from his cheeks, and his bright blue eyes sparkle under large white eyebrows.

"Don't you have any work to do?" he asks. "Is this what we pay our taxes for? You were snoring like a rhinoceros, Danielle," he adds chuckling. I'm embarrassed. He and his friends start laughing, fit to burst.

"Oh, go back to your game, you silly old fools," I reply, jumping up from the bench and this makes them laugh all the more.

I look at my watch and realise that I must get back to the office to meet up with David, so I straighten my uniform then leave with as much dignity as I can muster, to the sound of mock snoring ringing in my ears.

Chapter 13

After rushing to get back to my office in time for David, he arrives nearly thirty minutes late. I watch him through the window as he parks in the last remaining parking space which is, in fact, designated for the disabled. I don't want him to think I've been sitting here waiting for him to arrive, even though I have, so I open my notebook and begin to write and I don't acknowledge him when he enters my office. He stands in front of me for a moment or two before placing a bag on my desk. Then I look up at him.

"A peace offering," he says. "Sorry I'm late; I got held up."

"As in held up by a gunman or a robber?" I ask.

"Oh no, no, Danielle, just with stuff. You know how time can run away."

"Shame," I say and I smile.

He looks at me blankly for a moment then laughs.

"Ha, ha, very funny, I get it now," he says. "The bag contains two lovely apricot cakes. I know you like cake, Danielle, and I could murder a coffee."

"It's over there," I say, pointing to the table beside the sink. "Everything you need to make the coffees is there. I'll have mine black. By the time you've made them, I'll be finished this work and I'll be able to talk to you."

"Oh right, yes, I'll make the coffees then," he says and I return to writing nothing in particular in my notebook.

When we finally are seated with our coffees and cake, David begins, "About the parking, Danielle, I just don't know what to do. My tenants need to be able to park but the man who has an apartment in the next block has parked two cars in my designated spaces and he's gone to Paris for three months. So now there's only one space left and I park in it when I come into town."

"Forgive me, David, if I am wrong, but didn't you rent two parking spaces to the man?"

"Well not exactly. I rented him two spaces on the street, not in my parking bay."

"Well that explains everything, David. I've told you before you can't rent out space on a public street, even if it is in front of your building. I don't think this man has done anything wrong. He's paid for private parking and he's using private parking."

"So what you're telling me is that I can't have his cars towed onto the street."

"If you do, I will have to ticket his cars at peak times, and, as I'd know that you were responsible for creating the crime, I'd have to charge you, David," I reply.

"I guess I'm buggered then."

"I guess you are."

He sits sipping his coffee and staring straight ahead, deep in thought.

"I believe there was something else you wished to discuss with me," I prompt.

"Yes," he replies. "It's about this business at the apartment." He sucks in his mouth as if he has a sour taste in it.

"You mean about Monsieur Gold?" I ask and he glances away from me then nods in agreement. "You mentioned Mark before, is it something to do with him? Why was he at the apartment block in the first place?"

"Well," David begins, "when Mark thought his apartment was sold, he needed to empty his stuff from it, so I rented him my basement storage room, but of course the sale fell through. He was picking up some of his things when he saw me in the corridor. I told him that Steven had just gone upstairs, so he stopped what he was doing and went to speak to him. Mark was very angry with Steven because he was counting on the money from the sale."

"Where were you at this time?" I ask.

"I was in the hallway of the apartment block. I was hanging around waiting to show an apartment to potential tenants."

"So you could hear Mark and Steven," I say.

"Oh yes," he agrees. "Every word."

"Please go on."

"Well," he continues. "It was all rather embarrassing. As I said before, Mark was extremely angry. Steven didn't give a damn. He was practically dismissing him. Mark was going on about how Steven had taken a deposit from the potential purchasers of nearly 15,000 euros but not passed it on to the notaire. Steven was saying it didn't matter to Mark as it wasn't his money anyway. Then Mark said that of course it was, as the deposit was his security against the deal falling through, which in fact it had. Then Steven offered to give him 1500 euros of the money and he said the rest was his commission anyway. Mark went ballistic."

"I'm not surprised," I say. "It all sounds rather illegal to me."

David continues, "Things got really nasty. Mark tried to blackmail Steven. He said he knew all about Steven's wife and he would tell everyone what she was really like and who she was in her past life."

"Her past life, what did he mean by that?"

"Well," says David, "it seems that Madame Gold is not what she purports to be. She's not Hungarian royalty. She's not even Hungarian. According to Mark, she's an ex-prostitute from Albania who'd been working just over the border in Spain. He said he would tell everyone about how Steven met her on the internet when he was searching for internet sex."

"How did Mark know this?" I ask. I'm rather shocked by the sordidness of it all.

"Sheer bloody coincidence," David replies.

"Mark was scouring the net one night and came across her website. It seems that, before she met Steven, she was Madame Lash and she had sexy photos of herself on the internet. Mark is into all that bondage stuff. Funnily enough, Steven had never seen this website. He'd got her email address from a dating site. She'd removed her own website by the time they'd become serious about each other. But Mark recognised her."

"Oh, my goodness," I say. "I'm so surprised. It just goes to show you, you don't really know what goes on in other people's homes, do you?" I try not to show him how shocked I am but my heart is pounding in my chest and I'm sure my cheeks are burning. "Please continue, what happened next?"

"I heard Steven roar with rage. He was screaming at Mark and he said he would ruin him. Then he threatened to harm Elizabeth and the baby. He said they could disappear one night and nobody would ever find them. That's when Mark said he was going to kill Steven."

"What?" I say, "You actually heard the threat?"

"Oh yes," David says. "He said, 'you come anywhere near my family Steven and I'll kill you with my bare hands.' Mark is a big bloke with a nasty temper, I think; if provoked, he probably could kill him. I heard Steven laughing at Mark and calling him a useless little prick. Then the people turned up for the appointment and I had to go and I didn't hear anything else. Do you think any of this is important?"

"To be honest, David, I'm not really sure. I'll have to think about what you've said. I might have to get you back in to sign a statement."

"Promise me, Danielle, that you won't breathe a word of this to Mark or I'll deny everything. Although he's my friend, he can be quite intimidating and I don't know how he'll take it if he thinks I'm telling tales about him."

"Everything you tell me is private. You have no need to worry," I assure him. "I'll be in touch if I need to speak with you again but be assured, I will be discreet."

He stands to leave, and as I show him to the door, I scold, "You've parked in a disabled bay, David, but I'll let you off this time. Please don't do it again."

He laughs and walks off shaking his head and I know my words will go in one ear and out the other.

Chapter 14

I am rather stunned by what I've just heard. All this sleaze in one small town, whatever would my mother say, I wonder. I know I should be typing up the statements from Alan and Charlotte and also from David, but I can't concentrate and I don't know where to start. I've been bombarded with too much information in too short a time and I need to gather my thoughts. I decide, instead, to close the office and give myself the rest of the day off.

As I leave, I see my reflection in the window and feel uncomfortable about the person who looks back at me. My hair is too long and has grown out of its style. My body looks lumpy in the shapeless uniform. I'm dining with Byron tonight in a fancy restaurant and I need to smarten up.

I decide to visit the hairdresser in Ceret. The town is a lot larger than this one and a bit more up-to-date. The people who work in the shop are less likely to judge me or talk about me. I don't suppose anyone will even recognise me. I go straight to the hairdresser, instead of first going home to change, as I don't want my mother asking me a load of questions. She wouldn't understand or approve of me closing the office early but I'm rapidly running out of day. I also want to visit a clothes shop before closing time so I can buy a new blouse. I have a pair of smart black trousers at home, but nothing new or stylish to wear on top and the only skirt I own is the one I use for funerals.

I am uncharacteristically nervous about my 'date' as I like Byron and I don't want to seem gauche. When I arrive at the hairdresser, she says she can fit me in right away. It didn't occur to me that I might need an appointment. The hairdresser, whose name is Angela, is lovely and she's kind to me. I think she realises that I'm not sure what to ask for so she makes suggestions which she says will flatter my face. When it's finished and I look in the mirror, I hardly recognise myself. The hairstyle is short and spiky but feminine; Angela suggests that I also purchase some makeup from the range she stocks to enhance the look.

I leave the shop feeling like a million dollars. Angela has helped me to apply the makeup and it's made such a difference. Just a little mascara and lipstick has really improved my overall look and I'm thrilled. Now for the clothes, I think as I jump into my car and race back to town with just half an hour left until close of business.

When I arrive at the clothes shop, it's all rather daunting to me and I don't know which rails to look at or how the sizing is laid out. Marie, the owner, is here and I'm glad that I'll be served by her and not by her assistant who I find rather aloof. Marie is a little bird of a woman who is always busy and bustling about. She has great fashion sense and I'm sure her advice will be sound.

"Hello, Danielle," she says and studies my hair and makeup. "You look lovely. Special occasion, or are you here in an official capacity?"

"I'm not here on police business today, Marie," I reply. "I need something pretty to wear for tonight. A handsome English gentleman called Byron is taking me to dinner."

"Lucky girl," she says. "I know the man and he's very charming."

Marie lifts out two different tops to show me then she suggests I try on a simple, black dress. The dress really shows off my figure as it has a wonderful cut. I can't believe the person smiling back from the mirror is really me.

I hadn't intended to buy a dress, but Marie assures me that a little black dress is essential and something every woman should own. She says it's never out of place and can be worn for many different occasions. Marie shows me how to change the look of it with simple accessories like a piece of jewellery or a scarf.

"I hope I can pull this dinner off," I say nervously. "I've never been to a classy restaurant before and I'm not sure how to act."

"Just be yourself," Marie reassures me. "You're a lovely girl and your manners are excellent."

"But how will I know what wine to order?" I ask.

"Don't worry, Danielle, that's not your problem as it's customary for the gentleman to order the wine."

"What about food? What if I accidentally order something I dislike?

"Once again, let the gentleman order for you both, then if he gets it wrong, it's his fault and not yours," she says reassuringly.

I'm grateful to Marie for her help and advice and I now feel more confident about the dinner. I know the air is expected to be cold this evening, so I purchase the dress together with a pretty red scarf to wear at my throat and I can't thank Marie enough for her help and advice. As I drive home, I keep grinning like an idiot because I am so pleased with myself.

Chapter 15

I park my car in the lane adjacent to the spa then run up the steep stone steps to my street. My home is in the oldest part of town. This place was once only a village with a hot spring bubbling out of the ground but gradually the whole town grew around it. Once word got out that the spring had magical, medicinal powers, everyone wanted to live here.

My street has only ten houses and they form a sort of circle with a cobbled area in the middle. Most of the houses share adjoining walls but some face forwards and some face back and some are side on to the house next door. There are two narrow lanes that nothing bigger than a wheelbarrow can fit through and everyone has a tiny garden.

It used to be black as pitch at night, but five years ago the mayor agreed to extend the municipal lighting to our street and it has been seen as a mixed blessing. Before the lighting, it was dangerous to walk at night, particularly in the winter, as you could slip and lose your footing on the cobbles and there were no railings to stop you from tumbling down the steep slope. Now people complain that light pollution has stolen the stars from the sky and they feel part of the town instead of part of the mountains.

When I arrive at my house and open the door, which is never locked, I'm hit by a wave of heat and the smell of wood smoke from the stove. I quickly and quietly enter the house and go straight to my room to deposit my dress as I don't want my mother to see it until I'm wearing it. When I return back downstairs, my mother calls to me.

"Is that you, Danielle? I didn't hear you come in."

I enter the kitchen and suddenly remember that I haven't told my mother I'll be eating out tonight. The simmering pots on the stove show me that she's prepared a lot of food and I hope it's something that will keep until tomorrow.

"Dinner is ready," she says without looking up. "As soon as your father gets home we can eat."

"I'm so sorry, Mama. I meant to telephone but today was very difficult and I forgot. I'm having dinner with a friend tonight, so I won't be eating here."

She looks up and I can see the annoyance on her face. Then she notices my new look.

"What on earth have you done to yourself?" she asks. "I hope you haven't been wearing that rubbish on your face to work, what will people think? You are an officer of the law, not some cheap slut."

I shrink at her venomous attack but I'm used to her cruelty. I used to think my mother was always right about everything, and everyone says she's a good, god-fearing, pious woman. However, I now realise that instead of giving me advice and support, she's always criticised me. She's jealous of my youth and my opportunities and she's jealous because my father is proud of me and praises me. Even with this knowledge, her words always wound me and destroy my confidence, but not tonight. Nothing she says can hurt me tonight as I feel too happy. I don't wait for another verbal slap but instead go straight upstairs to wash and dress.

It's almost time for Byron to arrive when I return downstairs. My father hasn't reached home yet and I know he's probably popped into a bar to have a glass of Ricard with his friends after work. My mother will be annoyed as she hardly ever goes out and is lonely and bored. She has only her spitefulness and criticism for company and I wonder if she's always been this way.

She eyes me up and down as I step into the room. "Who are you dining with?" she asks.

"Just a friend," I reply.

She looks at me suspiciously, "Is your friend male or female?"

"If you must know, my friend is a man," I say, and I wait for a cutting remark. I'm very surprised when instead of acid her reply is sweet.

"Your father would approve of that dress," she says, not quite able to pay me a compliment herself. "I had one quite similar when I was a girl. I had a neat figure like yours."

I hadn't ever imagined my mother as a young woman and I wonder if she wore makeup or pretty clothes and, if so, what changed her? She's not old, being only fifty-nine, but she has adopted the look of one of the elderly ladies of the town. She wears a shapeless black shift over a plain white blouse and her grey hair, which is pinned up in a tight bun, has never, in my memory, ever been coloured.

I look at my mother and wonder if my father has made her this way or if it's simply the pressures of small town living. One thing I know for sure, I want my life to be different. It is strange how one event, one small change, can alter a person's perspective. We hear a car pull into the lane and both my mother and I go to the window and, as we peer through the glass, we see Byron step out of his vintage, Bentley convertible.

"Pah! He's not a date," she exclaims. "He's as old as me. I didn't think that a daughter of mine would end up a rich, old man's whore."

"I never said I was going on a date," I reply. "I said that I was meeting a friend for dinner."

I grab my coat and handbag and rush out of the door in time to meet Byron before he reaches my house as I don't want to give my mother a chance to ruin my evening with her poisonous tongue.

When he sees me, he says, "Wow, Danielle, you look gorgeous," and I smile at him and I believe him because, in his eyes, I am.

Chapter 16

Byron opens the door for me and I climb into the car and sink into the seat. The interior smells of polish and leather and money. Byron is impeccably dressed. He is clean cut and his shirt is white and crisply ironed, his shoes are polished to a mirror finish and he smells of lemon and bergamot. I find myself grinning with delight, like a child on Christmas morning, because for the first time in my life I'm being treated like a princess and I like it.

My mother would say that I was forgetting my place and I should seek the company of my own sort of people instead of trying to reach above my station. But where is my place, I wonder, and who are my sort of people?

We drive through Maurellies and head higher into the mountains. As we travel, the road becomes narrower and narrower. It is a very dark night and the car is large. I'm scared of meeting another vehicle coming down the steep slope towards us as there will be very little room for us to pass.

To the right of me there's a wall of rock with great jagged lumps of stone sticking out from the mountainside. As we continue upwards we pass several signs warning about rock falls. I see the road is indeed strewn with loose stones and some of them are sizeable. To the left of the car is a dark chasm which falls from my vision like a bottomless pit. I know on the return journey this will be my side of the road and I hope that, by then, I'll have consumed enough alcohol not to care.

We've been driving for about twenty minutes along the twisting, turning route and there are no buildings other than the occasional wooden goat shelter. Then, as we round a corner, the road widens and I see an ancient stone construction which, at first glance, looks derelict. As we draw nearer, I realise it's actually well cared for and light streams out welcomingly from several small windows. Byron stops the car and gets out then he comes round to my side and opens my door for me. It seems we have arrived.

It's a cold, clear night and the view when I look down the mountain is a brilliance of sparkling lights from the houses and villages below. I'm aware of the sound of fluttering wings which surround me in the darkness and I'm startled by them.

"Bats," says Byron by way of explanation. "Do not be alarmed, my dear. There are hundreds of them up here but they'll not come near you. They have radar you see."

Whilst I have no reason to doubt that he's correct, I don't take any chances and walk briskly to the door. As we step inside, I understand why the restaurant is considered to be high class as it's filled with beautiful antique furniture and it has an air of opulence. We are greeted by the owner who guides us to our table. He sits us beside a window so that we may enjoy the view. The interior lighting is subdued and mellow. In the inky blackness of the night, the twinkling stars seem to merge with the sparkling lights of the houses dotted about the mountainside and I feel as if I'm part of the sky, and it's endless. It's as if I'm floating in a void and I feel liberated.

"May I order for us both?" Byron asks. "I know this restaurant very well and I'm sure my choice won't disappoint you."

"Thank you," I reply and I'm grateful because I wouldn't know what to order in a place like this.

The waitress approaches and places a basket of warm, fresh bread and a large jug of ice water on the table. Byron orders, "We'll begin with champagne. Then we'll have the charcuterie followed by the tomato and basil soup, then the boar."

"And the wine, Monsieur?" the waitress asks.

"Oh yes, we'll definitely have wine," Byron jokes. "Ask Phillipe to recommend something please. He's never let me down yet and he knows what he's got in the cave. Does that sound okay, Danielle?" he asks.

"It sounds marvellous," I reply. "But you might need a wheelbarrow to get me to the car if I eat all of that. I'm not used to eating more than one course in the evening."

"Ah, but the night is young and tomorrow is your day off," he says with a sly wink. "You'll have plenty of time to sleep it off."

I'm about to agree with him when I remember that I've cancelled my day off and I have an early appointment with Kurt for breakfast at nine o'clock. Two dates to dine in as many days, I think. If this continues, I'll be the size of a house.

Chapter 17

I feel self conscious in these opulent surroundings and fiddle with my watch strap and tug at the hem of my dress. I nearly always wear trousers and it's strange to be staring at my bare knees. As the meal progresses, I relax a bit more and Byron helps to put me at my ease by talking about familiar subjects. We discuss the theatre and all the latest films and, by the time we have finished our main course, over two hours have passed and our wine bottle is empty. I politely refuse dessert but he insists that we be served liqueurs with our coffees. When the waitress arrives with the coffee pot, she smiles at me and I return her smile.

"I do like your dress," she says. "Did you buy it in Perpignan?"

I'm completely taken aback; nobody has ever complimented me in this way before and, coming from another woman, it's especially flattering. I thank her and explain saying I bought it locally to where I live. I give her the address and she writes it on her order pad. I'm still grinning when she walks away.

"I told you that you look lovely," Byron says and smiles approvingly. Then he changes the subject and with a more serious note in his voice, he begins, "I'd like to talk to you about Belinda. Have you noticed how strange she's been acting since Steven's death?"

He has my full attention as I too have noticed her odd behaviour. In particular, she's been drinking excessively. I've walked by her many times, sitting outside the bar late into the evening, usually with her children hanging around begging to be taken home for their dinner. The Belinda I knew, when she first arrived in the town, always put her children's needs first.

Byron continues, "She is deranged with guilt."

"Why does she feel guilty?" I question, surprised at his choice of words.

"It was Belinda's decision to come here from England. She made David uproot the family and buy the apartment block. She said to me that she'd believed everything Steven told her regarding the income they could expect. Based on his figures, she was sure there would be plenty of money and she and David would have more family time. In reality, the figures were grossly inflated and life is a real struggle for them. They're close to bankruptcy, you know. I met her one night shortly before Steven's death. She was very drunk and she was fumbling with her car keys trying to unlock the door. Her children were crying and the older one, Emma, was trying to take the keys out of her hand. They were begging her not to drive. When I came along, they pleaded with me for help."

"How awful," I say. "I knew they had money worries but I didn't realise things had become so bad."

"Eventually, I managed to talk her into letting me drive them home. I gave the children money to have pizzas delivered and I made a pot of coffee for Belinda."

"Where was David while this was happening?"

"God knows. He's always busy, doing nothing. He certainly wasn't at home when we arrived and it was already after 9.00. The house was like a pigsty. There was no heating and rubbish was piled up everywhere. When the pizzas arrived, the children ate them straight out of the box because there were no clean plates."

"You said she is deranged with guilt. That's an unusual statement to make. Do you think she's having some kind of breakdown?"

"I'm very afraid that might be the case," he replies. "She started ranting about everything being Steven's fault. She said he'd sold them a pile of shit and destroyed her family and she wanted him dead. She actually admitted driving her car at him one night as he crossed the road. It was the night of the storm when the street lights were out. She said he managed to jump out of the way at the last minute. Then she laughed and said, 'Better luck next time.' Her hatred of him has been festering for months, and I hope I'm wrong, but I'm afraid she might have been instrumental in his death."

"You don't think he was suicidal then?" I ask.

"Steven? Suicidal? Not a chance, he had far too much to live for. I was with him that morning. We were having a little chat about a potential business deal and he was keen to get me involved. There was no possible reason for him to want to kill himself."

I already know that the 'little chat' to which Byron refers was much more heated than he cares to admit. He'd been overheard by Alan and Charlotte who've said he and Steven had a terrible argument.

"Perhaps his death was an accident and no one is to blame," I suggest.

"Perhaps," he agrees. "But there is a rather high railing on the balcony he fell from. If he wasn't pushed, it would have been difficult for him to accidentally fall. People who are enraged or maddened often have superhuman strength. I think it's entirely possible that even someone as slight as Belinda would have had the ability to push him to his death."

We sit in silence for a couple of minutes sipping our coffees and liqueurs.

"Do you wish to make a statement about what you've told me?" I ask.

"Oh God, no," he replies. "I just thought I should tell somebody, and you are it in our town, Danielle. You are the person one tells. Just use the information as you see fit."

"I wish my Boss held me in such high esteem, Byron," I reply. "I don't know how many times I've been passed over for promotion in favour of some man."

"Ah, that's no reflection on your abilities, Danielle. That's what we English call the glass ceiling."

After we finish our coffees the conversation dwindles and I know it's time for me to go home. Byron excuses himself to settle the bill and when he returns he hands me a rose.

"A beautiful flower for a beautiful lady," he says.

I smile at him and blush embarrassingly but I'm thrilled. It's a perfect end to a perfect evening.

Chapter 18

My alarm goes off at 7.30 and I wake with a start. I had intended re-setting it for half an hour earlier as I have an early appointment with Kurt at Corsavy, which is a twenty-minute drive from here. But when I returned from my dinner with Byron, I completely forgot. I quickly wash and throw on my uniform then head downstairs. No makeup today, I decide, although I put my lipstick in my pocket just in case I change my mind later. As I enter the kitchen, I smell the rich aroma of coffee and see that my father is tucking in to a large lump of baguette.

"Good morning, Danielle," he says.

"Good morning, Papa. Has Mama already left?"

He nods his reply and continues eating. My father is a man of few words, but words are not necessary between us as I know he loves me and I love him. My mother will have already visited the market to buy flowers before visiting the grave of my brother George. She does this every Tuesday before going to clean the church. My brother died of meningitis when he was four and I was two and my mother is still angry at God for choosing to take her beloved son, when instead, he could have taken me. She feels guilty at being angry with God, so every week she cleans the church as a penance. I wonder why she doesn't feel guilty about wishing me dead instead of George.

My mother loves flowers, yet I don't remember cut flowers ever be-ing in this house. When I was young, I once went for a walk with my father and picked wild flowers on the mountain. When I brought them home to my mother, she put them in a jug of water and left them outside on the window ledge. My father thinks flowers in the house remind her too sharply of George's funeral.

I hastily drink some coffee then race out of the house. I just have time to make it to the office to check the mail before leaving to meet Kurt. The man makes my skin crawl but I like his girlfriend Rosa and I am curious to know what he'll say about her.

Rosa is very friendly and approachable; she's vivacious and pretty and is always smiling. She never has a bad word to say about anyone and everybody likes her. When Rosa became ill with glandular fever, many of the women who live in the town handed in food or shopping and this sort of help is very rarely offered to a non-local. It's a measure of how much she's liked.

When I am in the office, I pick up a notebook and pen. I may or may not take notes but I will wield it as a symbol of my officialdom, so that there can be no misunderstanding the reason for our meeting.

Chapter 19

I arrive five minutes late. Kurt is seated at a table by the door, and as I enter, he stands and looks at his watch pointedly.

"Late night?" he asks.

I am immediately enraged. How dare he? I think.

"Some of us do not have the luxury of spending our days idly," I reply. "Some of us have to work to support the people who claim benefits."

He purses his lips then smiles, his steely grey eyes never leaving my face, and I'm furious with myself for rising to the bait. As I sit down, he signals to the waitress who immediately serves us coffee and croissants.

"Well, Kurt," I begin, "what is it you wish to tell me?" I want to get our talk underway so I can quickly escape this horrible man's company.

"Come, come, Danielle, surely, as I'm buying breakfast, you can give me the courtesy of your company for a few minutes to enjoy my food before I must speak."

I suppose he's right. I'm letting myself down with my bad manners. I nibble at a croissant, sip my coffee and wait. I resist the temptation to look at my watch because I know it will please him to see me rattled. After what seems an interminable time, he finishes the last of his croissant and wipes his lips with his napkin. He stares at me for a few moments before beginning.

"My Rosa is not the person you think she is," he says.

"Whatever do you mean?" I ask.

We were both in our apartments the day that Steven died," he continues. "Rosa had spent the night with me but then she returned to her own apartment to await the arrival of her son. When we met in the garden and saw the body, I was shocked by what I saw, but Rosa showed no emotion. She stared at the corpse in a detached way. Death doesn't affect her as it would affect you or me, Danielle, because you see, my little pigeon has already experienced violence and death, and she has killed before."

I am stunned by what he's said but I say nothing. I try not to show any reaction until I feel I can speak without emotion in my voice.

"You say she's killed before. Do you mean in an accident?"

"If only that were the case, but alas, it is not. Allow me to tell you about Rosa's past then perhaps you'll understand my concerns."

Kurt orders refills of coffee and we sit in silence until they arrive, then he begins.

"Rosa was born in South Africa and her parents were middle class whites. Her father was Dutch and worked for a large corporation, her mother Spanish. Rosa attended a prestigious university in the 1970s. During 1976, thousands of black students protested against apartheid. That year the children of Soweto refused to go to school and instead the black students and their supporters made their way to a stadium to hold a protest meeting. They were unarmed, but the police, armed with weapons and tear gas, barricaded their way. This action set off riots which left hundreds dead and thousands injured. The blacks were crushed like bugs."

"Forgive me, Kurt" I say, "but what has any of this got to do with Rosa?"

"Patience, Danielle," he says. "Why do women never have patience?" he snaps.

He glares at me for a moment then he seems to remember who he is with and he quickly regains his composure. I'm surprised at how much anger he has and how quickly it rises to the surface.

Kurt inhales deeply and smiles at me, his snake eyes cold and unforgiving. "Many whites, particularly white students, became active for the cause. They were outraged by the inequality. I suppose you get bleeding hearts in every country," he adds. "There were protests and riots and workers began to strike; it was a dangerous time for South Africa. Many people were involved in violence, including Rosa. She told me that, on one occasion, she and a friend witnessed a white policeman beating a young black woman with a stick and they ran to her aid. They set about the policeman and managed to wrestle him to the ground and remove his helmet. Rosa told me that she picked up a rock and pounded his face with it until he was dead. She showed no emotion at what she'd done. It was simply a fact of her life, like visiting the shops, or attending the theatre, and I am rather surprised by how damaged she is."

I'm shocked by what Kurt has told me and I can't find any words to say. We sit in silence for several minutes sipping our coffees before he begins again.

"Steven knew of her past. When Rosa first arrived in France, she was married to a Frenchman and she lived in a very wealthy part of town. She met Steven at a property show. He hired her to work for him because she speaks several languages and that was useful to his business. Then they had a brief affair, about the time when her marriage was breaking up. At some point during their relationship, she told Steven of her life in South Africa. When the affair ended, he began to blackmail her."

He pauses and stares into my eyes; it makes me feel uncomfortable and I cannot hold his gaze. This makes him smile and I cringe with embarrassment.

"There is a man who farms cannabis in the mountains. I can't tell you who he is or the location of his farm, but it is in a remote place. Steven was buying his whole production then selling it in Spain. He was forcing Rosa to co-ordinate his drug business and take all the risks. Because her mother was Spanish, Rosa speaks the language fluently. She hated being involved with Steven and his sordid business and last week she told me she had a plan that would enable her to break from his grasp. She said she couldn't tell me what her plan was as she didn't want to involve me with her problems. Then all of a sudden, Steven falls to his death. Now do you understand what this has to do with Rosa?"

"I hear what you're saying, Kurt, but do you really think that Rosa would be capable of cold-blooded murder? Surely the circumstances were much different on that other occasion, as she was trying to save someone else."

"I cannot say," he replies. "I don't know what she's capable of. That's why I'm telling you what I know. It's in your hands now."

"Will you make a statement?" I ask.

He stares at me for a moment then laughs, his steely eyes never leaving mine. "Are you mad?" he asks. "If Rosa finds out, I might become her next victim. If you mention my name, I'll deny everything. But there's one thing I'll say for sure, I'll not be going near any balconies," he jokes.

Kurt signals the waitress. "L'addition s'il vous plait," he says, and she goes to get the bill. I realise that our meeting is over. When I glance at my watch, I see it is now 10.15 and I must get to Belinda's house.

Chapter 20

The mountains look especially beautiful in the morning sunshine and, as I drive towards Belinda's house, I look down over the valley. I'm surprised and delighted to see an eagle hovering above the river. I often see vultures in this area, as there are many species of vulture in the Pyrenees, but to see an eagle is a real treat. It seems to hang in the sky suspended by an invisible thread, then suddenly it swoops from my view, perhaps to lift a fish from the river or a small creature from the riverbank in its great talons.

I often wonder what it would be like to live in a large town and not be surrounded by all this beauty. I think perhaps it would make me feel closed in. But small town living can also make a person claustrophobic, as everyone knows you and everything about you. If I receive the promotion I've applied for, I could be sent anywhere in the region. The thought of change makes me feel nervous as this town is all I've ever known.

I can't stop thinking about what Kurt has told me. Could Rosa really be a murderess? I cannot visualise the Rosa I know in that role. She seems so gentle and I've never even heard her raise her voice. I cannot imagine her ever protesting in a march. She didn't get involved in canvassing to stop the electricity pylons being placed in the mountains even though there were many local protest groups. The Rosa I know did not hand out one leaflet or graffiti one sign, so how could she have killed a policeman?

As for Steven Gold, I know he was involved with many business deals and I've heard he even had a second-hand car business. But drugs? I find that hard to believe. However, I reason, he was the richest man in town and he'd recently bought development land with cash, so perhaps it was true.

I can't see what Kurt has to gain by telling me about Rosa, unless perhaps, it's to steer me away from discovering something about him. As I look in my rear view mirror, I can see him driving behind me. He's almost touching my bumper, pressuring me to go faster. There's no room for him to pass me and I refuse to be bullied. I'm almost at the turnoff for Belinda's house but I don't want Kurt to see me heading there, so instead, I continue into town and pull up outside the newsagent. He roars past me in a cloud of exhaust fumes.

I give him time to distance himself from me before I turn the car and drive back to the road junction. It will be about 10.45 when I arrive at Belinda's house which is plenty of time for David to have left for the airport.

Chapter 21

As I walk up the driveway towards Belinda's house, I'm shocked by the conditions I see. The driveway is strewn with rubbish. There's an old tumble drier rusting beside the garage, two broken bicycles lean against it and there's a mound of unidentifiable pieces of plastic, metal and wood heaped beside that. The garden is overgrown and full of weeds and bits of paper, cardboard and discarded pizza boxes are caught up amongst the plants.

I press the doorbell but it doesn't seem to be working as I don't hear it ring. So I knock on the door and wait for a minute. I don't hear any sound of footsteps coming, so I knock again, then step back to look at the windows for some signs of life. The windows are filthy; discoloured voile curtains hang haphazardly over them. I see movement at an upstairs window and Belinda's face appears. She holds up her hand and signals for me to wait and within a few moments the door is opened.

"Hello, Danielle, do come in," she says as she heads through the house. "Please excuse the place but I've been so busy." Her voice trails off and I follow her through to the kitchen.

We sit at the breakfast bar and she hands me coffee in a chipped mug. The inside of the house is no better than the outside. I can't imagine a family living in these conditions. It's very dirty and there's a strange smell about the place. A heap of washing is piled on the floor beside the washing machine which is not in use and, judging by the size of the heap, hasn't been used for some time. The house is freezing and Belinda explains that they don't use the central heating but instead make do with the open fire in the lounge.

"The children are used to wearing lots of clothes and the fresh air is healthier," she explains.

I know Belinda has been depressed, but I realise from the state of the place that she must have been suffering for a long time. She suggests we move into the lounge and then clears a pile of papers and magazines onto the floor to make a space on the sofa for me to sit down. I notice that some of the papers have chewed edges from mice and I'm not surprised. I have no intention of eating or drinking anything in this filthy house and I abandon my full mug of coffee on the floor.

"It's so nice of you to visit," Belinda says. "I rarely have visitors these days, apart from the children's friends."

"You invited me to call on you, Belinda. Don't you remember?" I ask.

She stares blankly at me for a moment then her eyes light up.

"Oh yes, that's right. So I did. I wanted to talk to you about Kurt." Her eyes fill with tears and her face twitches with nerves. "He scares me," she says. "He's a dangerous man. Kurt is a Nazi but I'm the only person who knows it."

Perhaps Byron is right, I think, maybe Belinda is deranged. "Kurt is Dutch not German. The Germans invaded Holland. So Kurt cannot be a Nazi," I reason.

"You're wrong, Danielle. Kurt's father was a member of the Henneicke Column. He was paid to expose Jews. He hated Jews and loved the Nazis and he was instrumental in sending many people to their deaths."

"How on earth do you know this?" I ask.

She explains, "Three month ago I went to speak to Kurt as he hadn't paid the top up of his rent. The housing benefit doesn't cover the full amount and Kurt is supposed to make up the difference. I tried to be firm with him because we really needed the money. He laughed in my face and said he didn't intend to pay me one more centime. He said if I wanted the top up I could ask my Jew friend as he had plenty of money. He was drunk and he was ranting and banging about the room. I was very frightened. He told me about his father and said he'd had the right idea about how to deal with Jews and their supporters. He was standing in front of the door, blocking my exit, so I couldn't leave. I tried to calm him down and I asked him who he was talking about. I said I didn't know any Jewish people. That was when he said that Gold was a Jewish name and Steven had Jewish blood in his veins. He said the Jews stole everything from his family. He's so prejudiced, that in his mind, there can be no other explanation for Steven's success. He thinks Steven was involved in some sort of Zionist conspiracy and I'm sure he thinks I am also, in some way, involved."

"So based on this, you think Kurt may have harmed Steven?" I ask.

"Yes, oh yes," Belinda replies. "He hated Steven's success. He was so jealous of him. He knew Steven despised him and looked down on him because he'd called him a worthless parasite to his face on more than one occasion. It amused Steven when Kurt would become livid with anger. He could be a very cruel man you know."

"You say you are frightened of Kurt. Do you think he actually means to do you harm?"

"Remember at the funeral when Rosa came to speak to me?" she asks. "She told me Kurt had specifically asked her to tell me he was thinking of me. I'm sure it was some kind of warning."

I think what Belinda is suggesting is rather far-fetched and she's guilty of letting her imagination run away with her.

"I'm going to tell Kurt I've spoken to you," she continues. "I've already told him I hated Steven because he was the cause of the dire financial position we're in. I said Steven could never be my friend and the less I had to do with him the better, but I don't think Kurt believed me. He wouldn't dare touch me once I tell him you know all about his threats towards me."

I'm sure Kurt will simply think that Belinda is off her head, so I can see no harm in her speaking to him. Besides, there's always the possibility, however remote, that it might give her some relief from the terrible torment she's putting herself through.

"Have you spoken to David about this?" I probe.

"Yes, but he thinks I'm going mad and I should pull myself together. He has never confronted Kurt about the money he owes us, although he always says he will. He never confronts any of our problems. It's always me who has to sort things out and I can't stand the pressure any more. I just want it all to end."

I'm afraid that I am inclined to agree with David; I think Belinda is probably nearing a complete breakdown. I feel very sorry for this broken woman as she's on the verge of losing everything. I decide then and there to contact Social Services and enquire if they can offer her some support. I cannot leave this situation to become any worse as I believe Belinda may become a danger to herself and her family. She is teetering on the edge of a pit of despair and the slightest breeze will have her tumbling into oblivion.

I'm so relieved to leave her house and I feel a deep sadness as I drive back towards my office. I wonder how David can continue to function as if nothing is wrong, but, I reason, perhaps he is also depressed and putting their problems out of his mind is simply his way of dealing with them.

I've just turned at the junction when I see David's Range Rover driving towards me and I'm in two minds whether or not to signal him to stop. Then I remember that Belinda specifically wanted me to call on her when he was out of the house, so I continue on my way. Belinda's fear of David overhearing our conversation makes me wonder if perhaps he is not as amiable as he seems.

Chapter 22

When I return to my office, I find an email from detective Gerard waiting for me. In it he informs me that, with the meagre evidence his team has gathered, it's impossible to determine the actual cause of Steven's fall or to rule anything out. He asks me to review all the statements taken on the day of the incident and, if necessary, re-interview anyone connected to the case then report back to him. He says he has neither the time nor the resources to spare someone from Perpignan for this task as he has to deal with a far more important incident which has occurred in the city.

I'm thrilled because I'm finally being trusted with a major case. I'm finally being treated as a policewoman instead of merely a traffic warden or a filing clerk. If I do a good job, it will certainly help my promotion prospects.

Having already spoken to most of the people who were present in the building at the time of the incident, I'm one step ahead of the game. I've to see Mark this afternoon and Rosa for lunch tomorrow, but even without their input it is pretty obvious Steven's death was not suicide. The statements which have been made firmly point to him being content and mentally healthy. It is imperative I type up a report based on the new information I've been given. However, not everyone will be prepared to have all that they've told me recorded, so I must be very selective in my choice of wording.

I'm very excited by this opportunity and I'm desperate to tell someone about it. I'm now the investigating officer on the biggest thing this town has ever seen, but I must keep my news secret for now, in case I compromise the investigation. I make a fresh pot of coffee to sustain me as I type then I look in the mirror, which is above the sink, tweak at my hair and apply my lipstick. I'm very happy with the person reflected in the mirror, as that person is confident and attractive and that person is the new me.

As well as typing my notes, I make a chart clearly showing the timeline of the incident. This chart should make it possible to determine where in the building each person was at the time of Steven's fall and, once I speak to Mark and Rosa, I may find that each person may be able to corroborate the statement of another.

I am an intelligent woman and I was always top of my class at school. I was also always in the top five for every exam I sat at the police college. Now at last I'm being noticed. Perhaps the glass ceiling that Byron spoke of is finally beginning to crack.

I realise it will be better for my promotion prospects if Steven's death turns out to be an accident. The Board will be less likely to promote a woman to a senior post in a town where a major crime like murder has taken place. I've a responsibility to report the information I find, but deciding what is true and what is relevant is entirely up to me and, at the moment, there is much conjecture but little evidence.

I glance at the clock on the wall and I realise the day is rapidly running out. It's already after two o'clock and Mark is due to arrive at three. The adrenaline is still rushing through my body and I feel ravenously hungry, so I telephone the pizza restaurant for a carry out and tell them I'm on my way to collect it. I should just have time to eat before he arrives. I really feel like something warm, stodgy and comforting and the slightly dried up baguette and cheese I have in my bag just won't cut it.

As I lock up the office and walk briskly towards the restaurant, I cannot help thinking that Steven's death has opened up a whole new life for me. The last few days have awakened in me all sorts of changes and opportunities and I make my way to the restaurant with a skip in my step and a smile on my face.

Chapter 23

I've had just enough time to eat my pizza and clear away the box when Mark arrives. I jump out of my seat to help him with the door as he has his sleeping baby with him and he's struggling with the baby buggy.

"Bloody Hell!" he exclaims. "You need two pairs of arms to get through doors with this thing. I've been rushing around like a headless chicken for two solid hours and this little bugger has been screaming blue murder and complaining all the way because he's teething. He's due to go back to his Mum soon to let me get on with work and now he's fallen asleep. Why couldn't he have done that in the beginning?"

I can't help smiling as I usher Mark to a chair. He is out of breath and his face is as red as his hair.

"Coffee?" I offer.

"No thanks, Danielle, but I'll have a glass of water if you don't mind. It might cool me down a bit. I didn't realise that babies were such hard work because he's usually with his Mum through the day. Elizabeth was up with him during the night, so I said I'd take him for a bit to let her have a nap. I'll not make that mistake again; I'm exhausted. I don't know how you women manage."

"Women are just better at multi-tasking than men," I offer. "It gets easier as the children grow up, because you become more confident and better organised, and they become more capable." Wise words from someone who has no children, I think.

"I'm sure you're right, Danielle, and I don't want to wish his life away, but I do hope this teething will be over soon. It's Hellish. He's in pain and we're exhausted."

Mark has been sipping the water I gave him, his face is less red and he's become more relaxed. He pulls a tissue from his pocket and mops the sweat from his brow.

"Now, you wanted to tell me something about Alan and Charlotte," I say and I open my notebook and take the lid off my pen.

"Yeah, yeah that's right. I don't want to be telling tales out of school but there are some things I think you ought to know."

He grasps his chin with his hand and thinks for a moment, then he runs his fingers through his hair and begins.

"I first met them through Steven. He arranged for them to view the apartment I'm selling and, rather than just give Steven the keys, I stayed in, so I could point out things like the wood burning stove and the state-of-the-art washing machine I'd installed. I'm really proud of the refurb I've done and I didn't want Steven to balls things up."

He has begun speaking to me in English and I don't want to ask him to change to French even though his French is very good, in case it puts him off.

"After the 'compromis de vente' was signed, or so I thought, I invited them to dinner at the apartment. Elizabeth had taken the baby to visit her aunt in the UK, so I was on my own anyway and I thought it would be a nice thing to do."

"That was kind of you," I say.

"They're teetotal, you know," he says. "Imagine that. They're planning to live in the most prolific wine producing region of France and they don't drink alcohol."

"That is unusual," I agree. "I don't think I have ever before heard of English residents who don't drink wine."

"Anyway, we're at the dinner table and eating a nice 'tranche de boef' with all the trimmings. I'm making small talk and I happen to ask them how they met. If I tell you, Danielle, that I was stunned with the reply, it would be the understatement of the year, nay the understatement of the decade." He raises his eyebrows and looks pointedly at me.

"Please explain. What did they say?"

"Well, she begins by telling me that Alan has been very ill. She says he was being given the wrong treatment and it nearly cost him his life. Then he cuts in and says that she saved him. Amazing, how lucky she was there, I thought, until she explains what happened. It turns out, he was in a nuthouse and she was a volunteer visitor."

"A nuthouse— what is that?" I interrupt. "I'm not familiar with that term?"

"A loony bin, a hospital for the insane," he replies.

"Oh, yes, I understand now," I say. "And she wasn't a relation but still she visited him. Is this a normal thing for someone to do in England?"

"I don't think visiting a nuthouse or a prison as a volunteer is very normal but many people do it nevertheless," he replies.

"Why was he locked up? Was he dangerous?"

"He was in the nuthouse because he'd seriously assaulted two people when he'd had one of his episodes, it seems. She told me he heard voices in his head and they told him to do things which he couldn't refuse. Well I tell you, Danielle, when she said that, I just wanted to get rid of them. I was sweating like a pig with sheer bloody terror. Here I was trapped in a third floor apartment with a complete nut job. What if a voice told him to stick me with a steak knife or poke a fork in my eye?"

"I can understand your unease and I too would have been nervous," I say. "But surely he's now on medication for his mental illness and it keeps him well."

"Well, Danielle, there lies the problem. It seems he was being medicated until they released him from the hospital. Then nutty Charlotte decides to cure him with bloody crystal healing or dowsing or some other off-the-wall treatment. That's why they're here. They ran away from the UK so the authorities wouldn't stick him back in the nuthouse when they found out he'd stopped taking his prescribed drugs."

"I thought their relationship seemed a bit strange," I say. "But I just couldn't put my finger on the problem. He does seem very mellow most of the time, unusually so."

"That'll be the cannabis," Mark says. "She says cannabis is a natural healer. So basically a serious nutter is being self-medicated with mind altering drugs. It doesn't bear thinking about does it?"

"Do you know who's supplying him with the drugs?" I ask.

"Seemingly, it was Steven. As far as I know, he was supplying everyone from here to the Costa del Sol. So it's rather unlikely that Alan or Charlotte would have hefted him over the balcony, but who knows what Alan is capable of in moments of madness."

"Alan told me Charlotte was a healer, but I assumed she was some sort of approved medical person," I replied. "Charlotte said Alan was a carpenter, and he expected to get work here, but I had no idea they were not as ordinary as they portrayed themselves to be. Don't worry, Mark, I'll keep an eye on them and I'll send an email to England and see if there are any warrants out for him. I do think it would be much safer for us all if they moved on somewhere else."

"Thank you, Danielle, I knew you'd understand. It's just a shame that they were the only potential buyers for the apartment and now, with Steven gone, who knows when another will come along. The man was a real bastard but he knew how to sell."

"What happened at your appointment with the notaire?" I ask.

"It was a bloody waste of time just as I thought it would be. Steven did receive the deposit from Alan and Charlotte and the bank manager has confirmed to the notaire that the money was lodged in his account. Then everything goes to pot. The' compromis de vente' which they signed was produced by Steven and not by the notaire. In other words, it's a worthless piece of paper which wasn't even a proper receipt. Basically, all it says is that they've paid Steven a fee for finding a property for them and assisting them in their purchase of that property. It wasn't even witnessed. It's been very carefully worded so that Steven could extract their money from them and keep it, no matter what, whether the transaction concluded or not. He was a lying, cheating bastard, Danielle, and he has royally screwed us all."

"Surely the notaire can do something? It all sounds fraudulent to me."

"He told me I have no claim on the money as there was never a 'compromis de vente' in my favour, so technically the money was not a deposit. He also said that Alan and Charlotte shouldn't have signed anything without first being able to read and understand it. They simply signed the paper Steven gave them without first getting it translated into English. Once again, the money paid was not technically a deposit, but a payment for services which arguably they did receive."

"That's terrible," I say. "So the money goes to the widow."

"Yeah and she doesn't even need it. She's loaded now that Steven's dead."

"You must be very upset, Mark," I console.

"Upset? You bet I'm upset. I tried to have it out with him you know. I was at the Carter's apartment block the day he fell. I was there to collect some of my stuff from the store room when I saw him heading up the stairs with a 'for sale' board and his tool box. We had a right slanging match and I'm sure half the street heard us yelling at each other. And I must say, at that precise time, I did wish him dead, but I didn't expect him to oblige me."

The baby begins to stir in his buggy and Mark springs to his feet.

"Got to go, Danielle, I must get this young man home and offload him on his Mum before he starts screaming again. I couldn't stand another session like this morning. Thanks for the chat, I appreciate it."

I usher him to the door and help him to get the buggy outside, then I smile to myself as he sprints along the street towards his home. Mark obviously doesn't have anything to hide or he wouldn't have told me about his run in with Steven. I believe that he knows nothing of how he died. I make some brief notes in my book before putting it away in a drawer then I gather up my things and leave my office. I plan to go back to the dress shop and buy some new clothes. I hardly ever spend any of my wages on myself but that's going to change. I feel as if I'm being reborn into a new improved me and I am excited to see how I turn out.

Chapter 24

It's 7.00 on Wednesday morning and the sky is just becoming light. I'm dressed in shorts, t-shirt and my running shoes and I'm waiting outside the café in the main street for my friend Patricia to arrive. We missed our usual session at the gym yesterday because I ended up working, so we're going for an early morning run today instead.

Patricia has been my friend since junior school where we were always the odd ones out. I was excluded from the groups of giggling girls because I was clever and shy. They called me names and ridiculed me because of the old-fashioned clothes my mother made me wear. If it wasn't for Patricia, I would have had no friends.

She, on the other hand, was bullied because she was tough. Patricia was the class tomboy and she was stronger than most of the boys. She feared nothing and no one. When the other girls would reduce me to tears, Patricia would always be there to defend me and comfort me. When she became a teenager, she was singled out and excluded because of her sexuality. Patricia didn't deny or try to hide that she was a lesbian. Having been sexually abused by one of her alcoholic mother's lovers, nobody could blame her for turning away from men. However, she once told me that she'd always known she was gay because she'd never fancied men and had always been sexually attracted to women.

From being the school tomboy, Patricia has developed into a beautiful and gentle woman. She is tall and slim and her figure is curvy without being over voluptuous. People always particularly notice her bright blue eyes, accentuated because her hair is dark, almost black, in fact. When she laughs, she has a way of throwing her head back and her eyes sparkle like sapphires.

I love Patricia and she loves me; our close friendship has endured many ups and downs. She's the only person I completely trust. I've never had a boyfriend or, for that matter, a girlfriend and I find it difficult to contemplate having a physical relationship with anyone as I'm rather frightened of having to give up control. I tend to keep myself contained and separate from people because I can cope better if I keep them at arms length. Patricia and I are as close as two friends can be because I trust her never to hurt me. We have recently been discussing the practicality of sharing a house. The only thing that's putting us off is worrying about the reaction of people living in this town. They'll immediately assume we are living together as a lesbian couple and that might harm my position as a police officer.

We both earn good wages and we spend a lot of time together as we enjoy the same things. Patricia is desperate to get away from the noisy family she rents a room from, and I'm desperate to escape from my depressing mother, so it would make sense for us to share. Besides, sharing a place will make things like paying the bills or buying food much more affordable.

When Patricia arrives, we set off at a steady pace towards the bridge. We usually head for the large village which is situated across the river. Then we run one circuit round it before returning. The round trip takes approximately forty minutes which leaves us both enough time get home, shower and dress before going to work.

As we run, we come upon a small house which is almost at the end of the village, at a point where there are great views. The house has quite a lot of ground around it; there's easily enough room to park two cars and still leave considerable outside space. The shutters are closed over the windows and the garden is rather overgrown but it looks to be in fairly good condition. There is a new looking 'for sale' sign attached to the metal garden gate and we stop our run to look at it. The sign is not from an estate agent but instead seems to be home made.

"I wonder how much they want for this house," Patricia says. "It's out of town and away from prying eyes but we could still both walk to work from here."

"We've always talked about renting together, but I suppose if we could find something cheap enough we would be better off buying," I reply. "And you're right, it is far enough out of town without being inaccessible."

"Do you think we could get a mortgage?" Patricia asks. "Perhaps it'll be difficult for us because we're females and we're both single."

"I think I can organise one through my union," I reply. "In England, many young people buy their own homes, even before they're married or have a family, so why shouldn't it be the same here? We're all part of the same European Union now. I'm sure if I applied for a mortgage through the city office it would be granted. I think in the city people are more up to date with their thinking. There are also schemes to help police officers to buy a home close to where they work and there's no reason why I shouldn't qualify. They can't discriminate against me for being female. I've a good income and secure employment."

"Shall we knock on the door and see if anyone's in?" Patricia suggests. "Perhaps we could ask to see inside and maybe find out how much they want for the house." She grips my arm; she's smiling and animated, and her excitement is infectious.

We enter the garden through the unlocked gate and knock on the door but we're not really surprised when there's no answer as the house looks uninhabited. Neither of us has a pen or paper as we're dressed for running and don't have our bags with us. So we agree that Patricia will come back here during her lunch break and copy down the phone number and, if she has time, telephone for further details.

We're really excited as we run back and we can think of nothing but the little house. Our entire conversation is speculating about what it would be like to live there together. We cross back over the bridge and go our separate ways but not before arranging to meet in the bar later to discuss the house and our future plans. I am full of excitement at the prospect of finally escaping my mother's strict regime. The very thought of it gives me a rush.

Chapter 25

I'm walking briskly along the street; it's still not fully daylight and there's hardly anyone around at this time of the day. Anyone who is out and about is either at the small market in the square, the boulangerie to buy baguettes, or they're already working. A bin lorry is in the street emptying the large recycle bins which are positioned alongside the shops. There's hardly a sound apart from a metallic screech as the lorry hoists the bin high into the air, then several thumps caused by the lid banging as the mechanism shakes the bin to empty it of its contents.

I feel invigorated from my run and the early morning air doesn't chill me. I allow my mind to drift and think about how my routine would change if Patricia and I moved in together. Patricia is a wonderful cook who likes nothing better than shopping for good quality produce and then preparing excellent meals. But as she is lodging with a large family, she rarely gets the chance, and instead she has to eat what is on offer. I, on the other hand, hardly ever cook as my mother does everything in the kitchen and has never encouraged me to help her. My father has taught me to do practical work, like sawing logs for the stove and repairing things around the house and he's also shown me how to catch fish in the river, so I would be bringing some skills to our partnership.

I'm hoping and praying that the house we've seen is affordable and suitable because, in my mind, we're already living there. I imagine that I'm growing vegetables in the garden for Patricia and she's cooking them on the stove, which is fired by the logs I've cut. I daydream that we're sharing things that give us pleasure, like working out at the gym, or staying home to watch the programmes we want to see on television.

Suddenly, I am shaken out of my reverie by the most blood-curdling screams I have ever heard outside of a movie. The awful sounds cut into the silence and reverberate off the buildings. My chest is heaving from the shock of those screams and I start to run towards the sound. I'm frightened because I don't know what I'm going to find, but my police training takes over and I act instinctively. I am outside the Carter's apartment block when I realise the source of the screaming is Rosa. She's in a state of near collapse and is on her knees on the pavement outside the building. She's wearing a flimsy wrap over her nightdress. Her hair is sticking out from her head as if she's just got out of bed and last night's makeup is still on her face causing black smudges around her eyes. I kneel down, grip her shoulders and look into her terrified eyes.

"Rosa, Rosa. Are you hurt?"

She continues to scream. I shake her to get her to look at me.

"Rosa. Are you hurt?" I repeat "Tell me what's happened."

She doesn't appear to be injured. Finally, her eyes focus on mine and she collapses against me sobbing.

"I've called for the pompiers," a voice calls down to me from the open window of the adjacent apartment block. "They'll be here soon. Whatever has happened to her?" the voice asks.

I look up and see that several people have their windows open and they're looking down at us. I'm aware that a slightly built boy of about eight is now standing beside us. He's wearing pyjamas and he has trainers on his feet. It's Rosa's son, Emil.

"Mama, Mama," he cries. "What's wrong? What's happened?"

I hear the siren begin to wail and I know that in a few minutes help will arrive.

"He's dead. He's dead." Rosa cries helplessly.

"Who is dead?" I question. "Tell me who is dead and where is he?" I give her shoulders a slight shake to get her attention.

"It's Kurt. He's dead. He's in my apartment and he's dead." She replies weeping uncontrollably.

She clamps her hand over her mouth as if trying to stop her words from spilling out as they're too shocking for her to comprehend. Emil begins to cry and tremble; the poor child looks terrified. I want to comfort him but I am frightened to let go of Rosa. An elderly man comes towards us. He is carrying the customary baguette tucked under his arm. He removes his jacket and places it around Emil's shoulders and stands with his arm around the boy. He asks no questions but draws the boy aside so he is no longer overlooked by the people at the windows above and for that I am grateful. I can hear the distant sound of the approaching fire engine and I know it will arrive shortly, and I'm relieved as I don't want to enter Rosa's apartment alone.

Chapter 26

When the paramedics arrive, one of them accompanies me into the building while another takes over the care of Rosa. We make for the lift only to find a notice taped to the lift door stating that it is no longer to be used. It has been condemned as the service contract has expired, presumably because of non-payment of the maintenance charge. Instead, we run up the stairs taking them two at a time. The paramedic is super fit and easily outruns me.

When I reach the second floor a moment or two behind him, he is standing on the landing not sure which of the open doors to enter. I remember from Alan's statement that Rosa's apartment is the apartment on the left and Kurt's is on the right. Rosa told me that Kurt was in her apartment, so we enter her door with extreme caution.

The paramedic, who is called Jean, follows me into the bedroom where we find Kurt in bed. He has pillows propping him up, an open book beside him and an empty wine bottle on the bedside table. His eyes are closed and he looks as if he's asleep. His colour is very pink and I wonder if perhaps he is just drunk.

"Open the windows quickly," Jean shouts. "And turn off the gas boiler from the central heating," he adds.

I run to do as I'm told as he goes to the bed to check for a pulse.

"He's definitely dead. I think it is carbon monoxide poisoning, probably caused by faulty venting from the gas boiler. That would explain why he's so pink. We should get out of here until the air clears. The poor man didn't have a chance. He simply nodded off and died while he was sleeping."

We shut the door when we leave the apartment and, as we descend the stairs, I ask Jean, "Was it an accident then?"

"It depends how you look at things. It could be negligence by the owner of the apartment, in which case it might be manslaughter. Or, if we find the device has been tampered with on purpose, then it could even be murder. But let's not go there for the moment. Once the doctor gives the okay to move the body I'll do a thorough investigation. I'll telephone you with my findings then I'll follow that up with a written report for your files."

I reach the entrance of the apartment building and I see that Rosa and Emil have been moved into an ambulance where a small crowd is beginning to gather. I give Rosa's details to Jean, as it is Rosa not Kurt who is the official tenant of the apartment. I also give him Kurt's full name and the Carter's phone number. I know I'll have to lock down the apartment as it is a possible crime scene so I ask the pompiers to make a call for me requesting assistance.

I wonder if, in some way, the Carters are responsible for what has occurred and I'm worried that this latest event will push Belinda completely over the edge. I'm happy I made the decision to telephone Social Services about her. Both David and Belinda will, of course, have to make statements and, depending on the outcome of the pompier's report, one or both of them may be charged.

I'm desperate to get home to shower and change into my uniform but I have to wait until another police officer arrives. I'm beginning to feel chilled as the perspiration from my run is making my clothes feel damp and there's a cold breeze blowing. Claudette arrives across the road to open her bar for the day, and when she sees me shivering on the pavement, she kindly lends me her jacket.

"What's happened here?" she asks. "Has somebody been injured, is Rosa all right? I see she's sitting in the ambulance."

"Kurt is dead; Rosa found him. It looks like an unfortunate accident."

I see no reason to conceal what has occurred as half the street heard Rosa's screams and it'll be better, at this stage, if people think it's an accident. I hear a police siren in the distance and I'm relieved that someone is coming and I'll be able to leave. It'll take me only a short time to go home and change. Then, when I return, I'll be able to take everyone's statements. I'm determined to keep control of this incident as it will help my promotion prospects. I allow the ambulance to leave with Rosa and Emil. They need to go to the hospital to be treated for shock and to check they're not suffering any ill effects from the poison. This also means that they'll not be available to answer anyone else's questions before I get to speak to them.

When the police car draws up, I see two young officers have been sent from Ceret to assist me. I explain to them that, as I'm now in charge of the investigation into Steven's death and as this incident has occurred at the same address, I can't rule out the possibility of the deaths being linked. I intend to take charge of this incident and I'll do or say whatever I need to make this case mine.

As it happens, they are delighted to leave things to me. They agree to wait for the doctor to confirm the death then they'll close up the apartment after the body has been removed and the pompiers are finished. It's an easy day for them as they can escape the boring job of typing and filing statements and all the other paperwork pertaining to the case. As far as they're concerned, the incident has happened in this town and it can stay in this town.

I've been advised that nobody will be allowed into the building until the pompiers are satisfied the apartment has been aired and confirm that there is no further risk of carbon monoxide poisoning. I estimate that I'll easily be able to make it home and back before then.

When I go to return the jacket to Claudette, I notice she's not missed the chance to make some money from this incident. Ever the opportunist, she has set up a table on the street and is selling hot coffees in paper cups to the gathering crowd. As I turn to leave, she winks at me and shouts a goodbye. I race towards home as quickly as I can, my lungs aching with the effort of running uphill. I don't want to waste a moment in case I miss something.

Chapter 27

I shower and dress at breakneck speed then I pick up my camera, a notebook and a sheet of plain white stickers before leaving the house. When I arrive back at the apartment block, Jean is waiting outside for me.

"The apartment is now safe but I've kept everyone outside so you could enter first with the doctor. The two officers you left here weren't very sure of the procedure in an event such as this, so I thought it best we wait for you as you're in charge."

The truth is that the other officers didn't want to have to write up the case so they've left the responsibility to me and I'm delighted.

"Thank you, Jean, that was most considerate of you."

I prime my camera and head up the stairs with the doctor and Jean. I don't have a clue what to do but I can't see any harm in sticking numbers on items, such as the central heating boiler or the empty wine bottle, then taking photographs and precise notes. My camera is able to record the date and time and, I reason, if I act as if I know what I am about then everyone will assume that I do. When we enter the room, the doctor goes straight to the bed and examines the body.

"Can you tell me anything doctor?" I ask.

"What would you like to know?" he replies. He sounds bored and mildly irritated.

"Perhaps you could tell me how and when he died?"

"This is not *CSI*, Madame," he replies dryly. "I do not have the facilities they have on television. I am a humble doctor, not a scientist."

I am embarrassed because I have demonstrated my lack of experience and I see Jean is chuckling to himself.

The doctor sighs then continues, "My personal opinion is that this man probably drank the wine from the bottle which is on the bedside table then fell into a deep sleep and, sometime after that, he succumbed to carbon-monoxide poisoning. That is why his skin is the colour of shrimp. There will have to be an autopsy because I believe he did not die of natural causes. You might wish to use that camera of yours to photograph the body and the wine bottle before they are removed," he adds. "Now if you will excuse me, Monsieur, Madame, I will arrange for the corpse to be taken to the morgue and I will await instructions from Perpignan."

Once the doctor leaves, Jean calls me over to look at the central heating flue.

"It is exactly as I thought, Danielle," he says. "Someone has partially blocked the flue with a towel and that has caused the build up of poisonous fumes."

"Why would anyone do that?" I ask.

"There have been strong winds recently and perhaps they've been causing the pilot light to keep blowing out and the heating to cut off. This system has been badly installed and I think it's likely that this is the case. By partially blocking the flue the pilot light would stay on and so would the heating. However, there would be nowhere for the fumes to go except into the room," he replies.

"So his death was avoidable."

"Oh yes, definitely. The person who blocked the flue killed him."

"So the cause of death was not accidental then?"

"Only if the unfortunate man himself covered the flue and did not understand the consequences of his actions. If someone else did it then it is manslaughter, even if they also had no idea of the risk. But of course, if someone did this with knowledge of the danger, then it is murder," he replies.

"If someone else had been in this apartment last night, would they too have been killed?" I ask.

"Most probably," he replies. "I cannot see how they would have survived."

I remember being told that, on the day of Steven's death, David was in this apartment because Rosa was having trouble with the heating and I wonder if he's had something to do with this incident. I don't know why Kurt was sleeping here alone. Why was he not in his own apartment and where had Rosa and Emil been? I have so many questions which need answering.

"If the flue was blocked a few days ago, is it possible that it would take this long for someone to be poisoned?" I ask Jean.

"We don't know when it was blocked. However, if the heating wasn't in use until last night, then there would be no fumes until last night," he replies.

If Rosa and Kurt had been staying in his apartment and not using this one until last night, then it's possible that David blocked the flue on the day of Steven's death and nothing happened until now, because the heating wasn't in use. However, that doesn't explain why Kurt was here alone last night.

I've taken several photographs and made lots of notes to study later. An ambulance arrives and I give the drivers permission to remove the body. Jean tells me he'll need a couple of hours to gather information for his report then I'll be able to close up the apartment. I'm very grateful to Jean for all his help and advice and I admit to him that this is the first time I've been involved in anything like this.

"I think you should email your initial findings to your superior in Perpignan and let him know everything is in hand," he advises. "Tell him you'll be forwarding my report and copies of the interview statements as soon as they're ready. Don't forget to inform him there's to be an autopsy," he adds.

I'm so pleased to have this advice because I now know what to do next. I shake Jean's hand and thank him profusely then we say our goodbyes and I make my way down the stairs. I speak to my colleagues and ask them to collect a spare key from the Carters then, when Jean is finished his work, lock up and seal Rosa's apartment. I've instructed them not to leave the building until everything is secure and everyone has left.

On my way to the office, I stop at the shops to pick up milk and croissants because I'm ravenously hungry and I'm feeling quite exhausted. It's now nearly lunchtime and I've had nothing to eat. I guess I won't be having Rosa's chilli for lunch today after all.

Chapter 28

When I enter the office I make straight for the coffee machine and switch it on. I'm eating the first of my croissants straight out of the bag as I'm too hungry to put it on a plate or to wait for the coffee. My mouth and my uniform are covered with the rich buttery crumbs but I don't care.

I see the light on the telephone answering machine is flashing, so I press the button to hear my messages. There's only one and it is from Rosa's ex- husband. He informs me that he'll be going to the hospital later today to collect Rosa and Emil and he's left his mobile phone number in case I need to contact him. He also thanks me for assisting Rosa and he lets me know that, for the next few days at least, she'll be residing with him and Emil. He leaves the address and I note that he lives on the outskirts of town in a very expensive area.

When the coffee is ready, I sit at the computer and try to compile an email about this morning's events. After forty minutes and several aborted attempts, I'm no closer to producing something suitable. I want my email to be formal and to cover all the facts but I'm too long-winded in my reporting and it makes me seem like the amateur I am.

The telephone rings when I am deep in thought and I practically jump out of my skin with surprise. I'm half-tempted to let the machine answer it in case it is Detective Gerard and I have to inform him of this morning's events before I get a chance to send my email. But after the eighth ring, I can stand it no longer so I lift the receiver and I'm relieved when I hear Patricia's voice.

"Great news, Danielle," she says, dispensing with the usual 'hello.' "I telephoned and spoke to the son of the owner of the little house. He lives in Carcassonne and he says he'll drive over here on Sunday afternoon to let us see it. Isn't that great?"

Before I can answer, she continues excitedly. "And it's cheap, very cheap. He only wants 60,000 euros for it. You can barely buy a one bedroom apartment for that amount of money. Can we get together after work to talk about it?"

"Yes," I reply. "I would like that. By then I might have managed to get this email sent. I've been working on it for nearly an hour."

"Oh, I'm sorry," Patricia says defensively. "I didn't mean to disturb you. I'm just so excited about the house."

I explain to her that she's done nothing wrong by phoning me. In fact I welcome the break to give me a chance to clear my head. I tell her about what's happened to Kurt and the problems I'm having trying to write my email in a professional way. I wish now I'd spoken to her earlier, because within a couple of minutes, she suggests the wording I should use and I type it into my computer as she narrates.

After making our arrangements to meet for a drink after dinner, we say our goodbyes and when I hang up the phone I reread what I've typed. It's perfect, I think, concise and formal yet imparting all the necessary information. I feel very satisfied with myself as I press the send and receive button on the computer, then watch as my email disappears from the outbox.

At the same time, I receive an email from the police in England concerning Alan. They're quick off the mark, I think, as I open it. I only sent my enquiry regarding him two days before. The message informs me that there are no outstanding warrants in his name but it doesn't rule out the possibility of him living here under an assumed name. It's not very difficult to create a false identity. He could simply obtain a copy of the birth certificate of a person who has died in infancy and who would have been around the same age as himself. Then the birth certificate could be used as identification when applying for a driver's licence or to rent a property and obtain utility bills. Armed with that paperwork, a bank account or an identification card may be applied for. Within a very short time, it's possible to build a whole new life on paper. However, Alan is not my number one priority at the moment. At least I've covered myself by making the enquiry. No one can accuse me of being negligent, and as far as I'm concerned, the matter is closed for the time being.

I look over my list of things to do and I think the time has come for me to contact David and Belinda and make appointments to interview them. As the owners of the apartment where Kurt has died, they have to be questioned about the faulty heating system. I do hope that it's David and not Belinda who answers the phone when I call and that Belinda does not go completely off the rails when she finds out what's happened. With much trepidation, I pick up the telephone and dial their number.

Chapter 29

"The Carter residence, who's calling?" David's voice sounds irritated.

"It's me, David," I reply, "Danielle."

"And what can I do for you now, Danielle?" he asks condescendingly.

He's definitely irritated.

"I'd like to talk to you about Rosa's apartment," I begin.

"Oh, let me guess," he cuts in with a sarcastic tone to his voice. "She's complaining about being asked to pay her rent perhaps, or maybe she's told you the lift's out of action. I didn't think either of these things concerned the police."

He sounds drunk to me and I try to cut in and tell him why I'm actually phoning but he goes off on another rant.

"I bet I know what you want. Oh yes, I bet she's been sticking her nose in where it's not wanted once again," he continues. "She's complaining about the noise that came from the apartment above hers, isn't she? She heard me and Steven's wife Magda having noisy, dirty sex and I bet she's jealous. Has she told you I threw him off the balcony because he found out about us, is that it? Well I can tell you I liaised with Magda only once and it was days before Steven was killed." He stutters over the word liaised.

I'm stunned by what I'm hearing and I try to gather my thoughts before speaking. "Is this true, David, you made love to Steven's wife and did he indeed find out about it?"

"There was no love involved," he snarls. "I fucked Steven's wife. I fucked her on the dining room table. I fucked her so hard the table jumped across the floor and she loved every minute of it. She was begging for it. She wanted me to fuck her and she was screaming for more. And yes, Steven did find out because that bitch Rosa told him. Can you believe it? She told him. What have I ever done to her?"

There is a pause in his tirade and he sighs audibly before continuing. "That bastard didn't care. In fact he laughed at me. He said I'd better get checked out at a clinic because she'd given the clap to better men than me. Then he threatened to tell Belinda all about it unless I sold my apartment block to his business partner Byron at a bargain basement price. He was a robbing bastard and I hated him. I'm glad he's dead. It's just a shame it wasn't sooner."

He gives another sigh and I think he's crying.

"I didn't know what to do. I'm sure he set me up so he could black-mail me. How could I be so stupid? I love Belinda. It's only ever been Belinda. But I didn't kill him, Danielle. I swear on my children's lives, I didn't kill him."

Oh my God, I think, where do I go from here? My face is burning with embarrassment and my discomfort is excruciating. I don't trust myself to speak without my voice cracking. I have never had to deal with such a graphic description of sexual conduct before and I find it particularly awkward because I know I'll have to face David when I interview him. Maybe this is what Rosa was planning to tell me today over lunch. I swallow hard then clear my throat.

"David," I say, trying to soften my voice. "This is not about Steven. I am afraid it has to do with Kurt. There's no easy way to tell you this, but Kurt is dead. He died in Rosa's apartment. I need to speak to you and Belinda because you are the owners of the building. Is she home, may I come round?"

"Fucking hell!" he screams down the phone. "Fucking hell! What the hell is going to happen to us next?"

I give him a moment to calm down. It is clear to me that he's more concerned about himself than about Kurt.

"I'm sorry, David, but I must speak to you both. May I come round today?"

"Oh my God, Danielle," he says. "Belinda has the car and she's gone into town. She was going to see Claudette. If she finds out what's happened, she'll fall apart. Please, Danielle, find her. I haven't got transport because she's got the car. I'm worried about her; please find her and bring her home to me. I'm begging you, Danielle."

I too am worried about Belinda, very worried. So I try to reassure David that I'll leave right away and look for her. He keeps apologising to me and telling me he has had a drink or two and I struggle to get him off the phone. Eventually I manage to hang up then I gather my things, lock up the office and walk round the corner towards the main street and Claudette's bar.

Chapter 30

As I walk along the street, I see Claudette busy putting two tables and chairs on the pavement outside the bar for the evening trade. It never ceases to amaze me that even in the worst weather, be it sub-zero temperatures or gale force winds, someone will use the outside tables and chairs so they can smoke while supping their drink. She looks up as I approach and nods a greeting.

"How are you, Danielle?" she inquires. "Nasty business across the street at the Carters. They don't seem to be having much luck do they? One wonders if perhaps they should sell up and go back to England."

"Actually, the reason I'm here is to ask you if you've seen Belinda today."

"Well, yes I have," she replies. "She was in here earlier and she was very upset. Someone had told her about Kurt. She was already quite drunk when she arrived and she was crying."

"When did she leave?" I ask.

"She's been gone for about an hour. She ordered a bottle of wine and she drank it all by herself. I was worried about her driving while intoxicated so I lifted her car keys off the bar. I have them here on the counter. I plan to telephone David and let him know I've got them."

"That was very responsible of you, Claudette. The state she's in, you may have saved her life and possibly the lives of others as well. Byron told me that once before she tried to drive while she was drunk. She doesn't seem to know when she's dangerous."

It is getting quite late in the day and the sky is darkening rapidly. I ask Claudette to inform David, when she calls him, that I'll continue to look for Belinda and I'll phone him if I find her. Then I leave my mobile number and ask her to get in touch if Belinda returns. I make my way down the road towards the café as I've decided to conduct my search in the two streets where most of the drinking places are to be found. I expect to discover Belinda in one of these establishments. When I reach the cafe I'm surprised that nobody remembers her coming in because it's the nearest place to Claudette's which serves alcohol. However, round the corner at the tapas, the owner does remember her and he says he served her with a jug of white wine. She must be very drunk by now, I think.

By the time I complete my search and return to Claudette's, I'm no closer to finding her. Although I've discovered that Belinda was refused alcohol at the nearby hotel less than half an hour before, because the owner felt she was already too drunk. So she can't have gone far, I reason. The bar has begun to fill up and I question the customers but nobody has seen her. I wonder where she's got to and I hope she doesn't come to any harm.

There is nothing more I can do tonight. I can't interview someone when they're drunk, even if I could find them, and Rosa's ex-husband hasn't yet telephoned to tell me that he's collected her from the hospital. As David, Belinda and Rosa are the only people I have to question, I might as well call it a night and go home for my dinner. I'm meeting Patricia in a couple of hours and I can't think of anywhere else to search. I telephone David to see if Belinda has returned home and he informs me she has not. He is quite belligerent and he sounds very drunk.

"You must keep looking until you find her," he demands. "She's a missing person and she's your responsibility."

"Excuse me, David," I reply. "Firstly, she is not a missing person until she hasn't been seen for at least twenty-four hours, and secondly, she's an adult and it's only six o'clock in the evening, so she can hardly be considered to be at risk. And as for being my responsibility, I've been doing you a favour by looking for her and you should be thanking me, not criticising me."

"Well fuck you, Danielle," he says. "You're no help at all. She could be dead for all you care. The children and I will find her ourselves. We'll walk into town for the car and then I'll drive around until I find her."

"You will not be driving tonight, David," I inform him. "I'm taking your car keys because I can hear from your voice that you're drunk."

"I am not drunk!" he screams down the phone. "You have no fucking right to take my keys. I'm coming to the bar for my keys and they'd better be there, you fucking lesbian cow."

He slams down the phone and I'm left stunned and shaken by his verbal assault. Claudette can see I'm upset and she pours me a small brandy on the house. I thank her and I swallow it down. Then I take Belinda's car keys and advise Claudette that I'll be in town later with my friend but she can call me if she has any trouble with David. She assures me she can handle David but promises to telephone if she needs me. It is with great relief I finally head for home as I'm extremely tired and it's been a very, very long day.

Chapter 31

When I arrive home, my parents are sitting at the dining table waiting to begin their evening meal. I would like to go and change out of my uniform, but the look on my mother's face, and the way she jumps up from the table to serve our food as soon as I enter the room, makes me decide simply to wash my hands and sit down.

"You are later than usual," she says accusingly.

"I'm sorry, Mama, but it's been a very busy day," I reply.

"So I've heard," she says grimly. "You were the talk of the boulangerie today. Everyone was commenting about the way you took charge of the incident this morning."

I'm delighted that I've been noticed, but if I expected praise I'm to be sorely disappointed.

My mother continues. "What were you thinking of, Danielle, pushing your way forward like that? I heard there were two male officers in attendance but you kept them outside while you took over. You should have stayed in the background and let the men do their jobs. You should have tried to learn from them because they probably handle these sorts of cases all the time. They'd certainly know more than you. What you did was unseemly and unfeminine and everyone is talking about it."

A plate of food is plonked down in front of me but I've lost my appetite.

"Do you feel the same way, Papa," I ask, turning to my father. I'm hoping for support from him.

"I'm sure you're capable of doing the job, Danielle," he replies cautiously. "But you know I've never been happy with you doing what I see as man's work."

My mother cannot hide the smirk on her pursed lips.

"I was embarrassed," she continues. "It would be different if you were married or even had a boyfriend, but people talk when you're over thirty, unmarried and doing a man's job. It's not normal for a young woman."

"Oh for God's sake, Mama," I exclaim. "I'm a qualified police officer doing important and difficult work, and doing that work well, I might add. I don't really care what the narrow minded bigots of this town say but I'm upset with you. You should be proud of me; I'm your daughter and you should support my position. I cannot bear your constant criticism. I spend my life walking on eggshells in this house."

"If you hate it here so much, maybe you should move away," she replies sharply. "Your father and I have always supported you, but this is our house and while you live under our roof, you must respect our feelings."

It suddenly dawns on me that she's right. It's time for me to move out of this stifling house. I'm an adult, not a child, and I've suppressed my desires and feelings for too long. Not wishing to get into a shouting match by pointing out that my unacceptable job contributes a very substantial part to the family budget, I rise from the table and go to my room to change. My mother's complaints about my dinner being wasted follow me up the stairs.

I dress carefully in some of my new clothes then I apply my mascara and lipstick. A confident woman looks back at me from the mirror and I know I can never return to the way I was before. I'm more determined than ever to find a suitable place to share with Patricia and I hope, when we meet tonight, she feels just as strongly.

I pick up my handbag and fill it with my make-up, my phone and some money. Then I grab my coat and quietly leave the house without saying goodbye. It is a relief to be out on the street and breathing the cool night air. I've arranged to meet Patricia in the café and I make for there now. I'm very early but I can grab a bite to eat before she arrives and calm myself with a little jug of 'vin rouge.' I feel full of hope for the future and our discussion this evening could mean a whole new life for me. It's as well my mother has pushed me to my limit, or I may have ended up spending my entire life miserable, under her roof.

When I arrive at the café, I sit at a table in the corner beside the window so I can look out for my friend arriving. The café is warm and bright and there's a buzz of conversation and a bustle of movement about the place. Within a few minutes, I am tucking into a bowl of piping hot rabbit stew and sopping up the rich gravy with thick pieces of freshly baked bread. The dark, heavy red wine is a perfect accompaniment and I relax and am warmed by it.

The waiter, who I have known for many years, pays me a compliment about the way I look and, although I blush embarrassingly, I'm thrilled. I'm finally being noticed for the right reasons and I wonder why it took me so long to grow up and become the person I'd always hoped I'd be.

Chapter 32

Patricia sees me as she walks past the window and she gives me a wave. When she enters the café, she comes straight over to the table.

"I see you've started without me," she says, nodding at my empty wine glass.

"It's a long story," I reply.

She quickly peels off her jacket and removes her scarf, which is wound round twice to keep out the night chill. She then takes a seat opposite me. I beckon to the waiter and order another jug of red wine and an extra glass. We briefly discuss my busy day and she is very sympathetic when I tell her about the conversation with my mother.

"All the more reason for us to look at the little house," she says. "I can't wait to escape from the noise of the family I lodge with and today I found that one of the children had been in my room because he left a toy car behind. When I moved in they assured me I had the only key but now I know they were lying."

"Are you absolutely sure you want to live with me now you know that, according to my mother, the whole town disapproves of me?" I ask.

"Hah!" she replies. "If you think they disapprove of you then what do you imagine they say about me? A thirty-year-old lesbian who challenges men and paints make-up on corpses for the funeral director, I'm a tough act to follow."

The wine arrives and I fill the glasses.

"Now about the house," she says. "I telephoned the number from the sign and the phone was answered by the owner's son. It seems the owner's wife has died and he's becoming too elderly to live on his own, so his son has moved him to Carcassonne to live with him and his family. He's looking for a quick sale and that's why the house is priced so low."

"It does sound very cheap," I agree. "We could easily afford the mortgage repayments and I personally would be a bit better off each month because I pay a substantial amount into my parents account for my keep. Did he say what sort of condition the house is in?"

"Well, that's the best bit, Danielle. He told me he had a new gas central heating system installed only two years ago as his mother was becoming infirm and was really feeling the cold. He also said that, behind the shutters, the windows are double glazed and the roof has been overhauled within the last few months."

"Wow," I say. "That takes care of all the expensive things. If we can manage to buy this before any of the estate agents get wind of it, we'll be getting a real bargain."

"I know," she says excitedly. "I can hardly believe it. I don't want to think about it too much in case we don't get it but, on the other hand, I can think of nothing else."

"What time on Sunday did you arrange?"

"Two o'clock. He's driving over after church."

We sit and chatter about our plans for the house and our new life together and within a short time we've finished the wine and I order another jug. There has been a constant coming and going at the café but my attention is drawn to the door when Patricia makes a comment.

"Would you look at them," she says approvingly. "Aren't they stunning? They're unusually beautiful and elegant for this old-fashioned town. Their clothes are fabulous and so up to date."

I look over to see Byron and Mark have entered and it is they who are the centre of Patricia's attention.

"I thought you were gay," I hiss at her.

"One does not need to like a fine sculpture to appreciate its merits," she says sniffily.

Byron and Mark notice me. They smile and wave then head over to our table.

"Good evening, ladies," Byron says and he takes my hand and bends to kiss it. "And how are you both this fine evening?"

We assure him that we're both well. He and Mark take their seats at a nearby table, and after ordering food and wine, they produce a chess game and begin to play.

"Are they suspects in your case?" Patricia asks.

"Not in this latest incident," I reply. "And I really don't think there's any evidence to prove their involvement in Steven's death either. I'm still compiling my reports but can we please change the subject? It's been a long day and I don't want to discuss work when we have so many more interesting things to talk about."

"Good," she says and nods in the direction of Byron and Mark. "They're too beautiful to be involved in something so ugly."

"I had dinner with the older gentleman, his name is Byron," I say. "He took me to a very posh restaurant and we had a lovely evening."

"My, my, aren't you the dark horse. Was it a date?"

"Don't be ridiculous," I answer. "He's old enough to be my father. It was simply me having dinner with a friend."

"Tell him the next time he asks that you have a friend who could join you. I wouldn't mind being wined and dined by a wealthy older man. As long as there were no strings attached," she adds, laughing.

We get back to our conversation about the house and we're feeling rather merry due to the copious amounts of alcohol we've consumed. When suddenly we hear shouting coming from the street outside.

Chapter 33

Patricia and I peer out of the window and we can see that a small crowd has gathered a short distance along the street. The shouting seems to be coming from there but we can't make out what's happening as it is very dark. Byron and Mark leave their game and come over to our table.

"Can you see anything?" Byron asks.

"There's some sort of commotion in the street," I reply. "But I can't make out what's happening."

Byron leans on the back rail of my chair. His arm is draped casually over the chair and his hand rests on my shoulder as he looks out of the window. It's an intimate gesture which feels comfortable. I'm aware that it crosses the divide between acquaintance and friend and I'd like this man to consider me his friend. Mark leans across the small table, cups his hands round his eyes and presses his hands to the window to obscure the light and get a better view.

"Oh my giddy aunt!" he exclaims. "It's Belinda. I think she's drunk. She's shouting at people in the street and swaying about."

"Belinda? Are you sure?" I ask.

"Yep, it's definitely her. We'd better get out there," he says to no one in particular.

Well at least she's turned up, I think. It's with great reluctance that I drag myself from my chair and join Byron, Mark, Patricia and a couple of other diners and head for the crowd in the street.

"Welcome to the house of death na, na, na, na, naa," Belinda is singing at the top of her voice to the tune of 'House of Fun' by Madness. "Who's next to die? Don't be shy. Oops, I'm a poet and I know it," she giggles. "Come on all you losers. I'm the kiss of death. Want a kiss?"

She reels towards a man in the crowd and practically falls on him. He backs away shaking his head with disgust.

"Roll up, roll up, only one euro to enter the house of death. Well, I have to get money from somewhere," she reasons. "Never mind Switzerland, anyone who wants to die can come with me, cheapest euthanasia in town."

"We'd better do something," Byron says, looking pointedly at me. "Perhaps one of us should drive her home."

"I am sorry, Byron, but I've had too much to drink," I say. The truth is that after the hurtful way David spoke to me, I want nothing to do with either of them unless it's purely work related.

"Well I'm not going to put her in your car, Byron, in case she throws up. It's a vintage Bentley, for Christ's sake," Mark states.

"Come on, you fucking losers!" Belinda is shouting and crying. "Who wants to stay in this pile of shit?" she shouts. She gestures with the wine bottle she's clutching in the direction of her apartment block. "I've got lots of vacancies. Short term lets available. Very short term if you die."

"I'll telephone David to come and get her, shall I?" Byron suggests. "He'll know what to do with her."

"I'm sorry, Byron, but I spoke to him a short time ago and he was very drunk. In fact, I confiscated their car keys in case one of them tried to drive and caused an accident."

"What shall we do?" he asks. "We can't just leave her here. She's becoming a rather nasty drunk. Look at her swinging that empty wine bottle at the people in the crowd. She might injure someone."

"Call the police," I suggest.

"But you are the police," he replies.

"Not tonight, I'm not. I'm off duty."

I know I'm being callous but I've had enough of this couple. They are lazy and they are stupid and I don't want to be involved with them tonight.

"Are you coming, Patricia?" I ask. "We have a lot to talk about and we still have some wine left. You can do what you like, Byron, but I'm going back to the café."

I take Patricia by the arm and lead her away from the spectacle. We head back to the warmth of the café. It's about time the people of this town stopped taking me for granted, I think. It's time I was allowed to have a life. After about ten minutes, I hear a police car approaching and I'm relieved when Byron and Mark return to the café. She's someone else's responsibility now, I think with relief.

"Everything okay?" I ask.

"Yeah, yeah" Mark replies. "The cops said we did the right thing in calling and they're dealing with her now. I'm glad we didn't attempt to take her in Byron's car because she threw up on the pavement moments before they got her into the police car."

"Thanks, Danielle," Byron says. "I'm sorry that I expected you to take care of her. It was very wrong of me. You are such a commanding figure in this town that it's easy to forget you have a life outside of your job. Please accept my sincerest apologies."

I nod my acceptance and I am thrilled that Byron sees me as a commanding figure. I hope the promotion board will feel the same way. Patricia and I stay in the café until well after midnight. Neither of us wants to leave because we have so much to talk about. As we finally say our goodbyes, she points out that, with luck, we will soon be saying goodnight while living under the same roof. This happy thought warms me as I walk through the dark streets, in the chilly night air, and walk towards home.

Chapter 34

My ringing alarm clock wakes me from a deep sleep. I'm so tired I feel almost drugged and I have difficulty hauling myself from my bed. A combination of excitement, stress, too late a night and a lot of wine all add to my feeling of exhaustion. I take a shower with the temperature turned to cool to try to rouse myself, but all it succeeds in doing is make me feel chilled, so I quickly put on my uniform and go downstairs for breakfast. My mother is washing dishes at the sink and she's giving me the silent treatment. I'm relieved because I don't have the energy or the inclination to talk to her.

As I leave the house and head for the office, I wonder what today will bring. I hope it will be less eventful than yesterday so I might have some time to recover and gather my thoughts. I know, at some point, I'll need to make a telephone call to find out what's happened to Belinda, but that can wait until later.

When I enter the office, I switch on the coffee machine as usual but add an extra spoonful of coffee grounds and hope the extra caffeine will help to wake me up. The computer is showing one new message and I click on it to open it. It's from my head office in Perpignan and it reads, 'Received your correspondence. Well done, keep up the good work. Promotion board will convene 30th March.' It's been sent from Detective Gerard's office.

Suddenly I'm wide awake and I'm thrilled. I must have got the email that I sent him just right to get this kind of positive response. As Patricia helped me so much by making suggestions for it, I telephone her at work to tell her my good news. Unfortunately, she's with a 'client,' her Boss tells me, but he says he'll give her a message to phone me back. He doesn't realise my call is personal because I give him the impression it's related to a police matter regarding a recent death. I don't want to get my friend into trouble, especially when I'm calling to thank her.

After I hang up, I notice the light flashing on the telephone answering machine and I press the button to listen to the message. It's from Rosa's ex-husband Raymond to inform me that Rosa is now at his home and he leaves the land line number for me to call. I jot down questions that I want Rosa to answer and, when I'm satisfied they cover all the information I'll need, I telephone the number he's left. The phone is answered by Rosa and she's pleased to hear from me. I ask her how she and Emil are keeping and she assures me that they're both all right although they are still very shocked and upset. I arrange to see her in half an hour to take her statement. She's relieved I'm calling on her as she just wants to get the whole business over with.

I am about to leave the office to interview her when the telephone rings, but as I don't want to be late I let the machine get it. If it's Patricia, I know she'll phone back and if it's someone else, they can leave a message. I take David's car keys with me so, if I choose, I can stop at his house on the way back and take his statement and hopefully Belinda's. Then I drive towards the richest part of town for my meeting with Rosa.

The estate is very impressive. Two stone pillars mark the entrance to the mono-blocked driveway and a very large house stands in the middle of landscaped gardens. It is freshly painted in gleaming white and the front façade has a wall of sliding glass doors. I've never been inside one of these residences before so I don't know what to expect, but as I enter, I see that nothing in my imagination could have prepared me for the opulence of the place. It's like a palace. Rosa offers me a seat on the sofa and I practically disappear into the soft, plush leather. She cannot seem to stop herself from crying and she constantly apologises for this.

"It's just the shock," she explains. "I can't get the picture of him lying there out of my head. At first I thought he was drunk. I still can't believe that he's dead."

I try to ease in gently by asking her about the house instead of storming in with questions about Kurt.

"Did you used to live here when you were married to Raymond?" I ask.

"Yes," she replies. "This is our family home. When we separated, I moved out and left Emil here with his father so he didn't have too many changes in his life at the one time."

"It's a lovely house," I say. "I don't know how you could bear to leave it. It must have been very hard on Emil when you left."

"There was no anger between Raymond and I, and Emil can see both of us any time he wants, so it hasn't been too traumatic for him. Raymond still loves me you know, and I love him. Emil is well aware of that."

"What went wrong?" I ask.

"Raymond has been having a relationship with someone else. It started before we were married. In fact they first met when they were at university together. When I found out, I realised that I couldn't live a lie and I couldn't bear to share him."

"How awful for you," I say. "Why did he marry you and not the other woman?"

"There is no other woman, Danielle. Raymond's other love is a man. Raymond wanted to have a conventional life with a wife, children, nice house the whole package but he couldn't give up Yves, although for a while he did try. It nearly broke his heart and I couldn't stand it, so I moved out. We haven't actually divorced you know, because, as I said before, we do still love each other."

"So that's how you became a tenant of the Carter's. How did you meet Kurt?"

"He lived in the block before I moved in and he was very kind to me. Then, of course, we became lovers." She hangs her head and mops her tears with a sodden handkerchief.

"You each had your own apartment. What was the set up there?" I ask.

"Kurt had a two bedroom apartment, but mine just had one bedroom so most of the time we stayed in his because it was bigger. But when Emil was visiting, Kurt and I exchanged apartments so that Emil and I could spend exclusive time together and Emil could have his own bedroom. I didn't think it appropriate for Emil to know that Kurt and I were lovers."

"So on the night Kurt died, he was alone in your apartment because Emil was with you in his."

"Yes, that's correct."

"Had either of you stayed in the apartment since David sorted the heating for you?"

She thinks for a minute before answering.

"We went in and out of the apartment to collect things but we didn't actually spend any time there and we didn't have the heating on. They told me at the hospital they were checking me for carbon monoxide poisoning. Is that what killed Kurt?"

"I think so, but it hasn't been confirmed yet," I answer truthfully.

She covers her mouth with her hand and in a whisper asks, "Could David have done this when he fixed my central heating? He threatened me, Danielle. I was coming to tell you about it then all this happened."

"Why did he threaten you, Rosa? What had you done to upset him?"

"I heard him with Steven's wife Magda; they were having sex. They were in the apartment above mine and I heard everything. When David came to fix the heating, he accused me of blabbing to Steven but I'd said nothing. Then he said that if Belinda ever found out, he would kill me. He was gripping my arm and he was raging; he practically spat the words into my face. It was very frightening."

"Where were you when he was fixing the heating?"

"The boiler, as you know, is in the cupboard in the bedroom, so I went into the sitting room because I wanted to be out of his way."

"So you didn't see what he did to the boiler."

"Even if I had, I wouldn't have understood anything as I'm not very technically minded. I always left things like that to Kurt."

She holds her handkerchief to her eyes and tries to regain her composure but a hiccupping sob escapes from her lips. I don't want to press her too much as she's obviously deeply upset but I have one more question that must be answered.

"Could Kurt have tampered with the system if the heating had gone out again?"

"Kurt used to fit central heating systems for builders," she says. "He could have easily fixed the problem but he said David was being paid to maintain the heating, so it was his responsibility. Kurt certainly wouldn't have made a mistake that would potentially kill him."

"I know this is a difficult question, Rosa, but would Kurt have any reason to want to hurt you?"

"No, definitely not. We were lovers," she answers emphatically.

I close my notebook and put it back into my bag.

"Are we finished?" Rosa asks expectantly.

"Thank you, yes," I say and I haul myself out of the very comfortable sofa.

She's relieved to have the interview over. As I'm about to leave, Raymond enters the room. He walks over to us and places a protective arm around Rosa's shoulders. I hadn't been aware of him being in the house. He is a very handsome man with fine features and a shock of beautifully styled white hair. He tells Rosa that he has run her a bath and she excuses herself, says goodbye to me, then leaves the room.

As Raymond sees me to the door, he says, "I think Rosa will be moving back into this house permanently. It's for the best. I don't want her anywhere near that apartment block or anyone connected with it. The place is a slum and the owners are trash. If you need to contact her again, she'll be here with me and Emil. This is her home and this is where she belongs."

With that, he shakes my hand and thanks me for coming and I leave the 'palace' and step back into the real world. I decide to head straight for the Carter residence while everything Rosa has told me is still fresh in my mind and, as I drive out of the grounds, I cannot help thinking that Rosa would indeed be better off staying here.

Chapter 35

As I drive towards the Carter's house I am dreading having to go inside. The last time I was here it was filthy, and I don't imagine it'll be any different this time. The contrast of what I've just left and what I'll be shortly arriving at couldn't be more pronounced, and I can understand why Raymond wouldn't want Rosa to be connected with David and Belinda in any way.

As I approach, I see the same rubbish strewn in the driveway that was there the last time and the rusting, broken heap of trash is still piled up outside the garage. It's with a heavy heart that I drag myself out of my clean car and walk towards the house. Usually, when I visit someone's home, I wipe my feet on the doormat when I enter, but on this occasion I am more likely to wipe my feet when I leave. I knock on the door because I remember that the last time I was here the doorbell was broken and I don't suppose anyone has fixed it. I hear heavy footsteps approaching, and a moment later the door is opened by David.

"Oh, it's you," he says. "What do you want now?"

I'm instantly rattled by his rudeness but I'm determined he'll not get the better of me.

"I'm here to interview you regarding the second death that has occurred at the apartment block you own with your wife Belinda," I say formally. "I can conduct the interview here or, if you prefer, you can accompany me to the police station."

Suddenly, the schoolboy charm returns and he says, "Here would be great, Danielle, if that's not too much bother. It's very good of you to come to my home and save me the journey into town." He beckons to me to come in.

I fish his car keys out of my bag and hand them to him as I don't want to find myself half way back to town with them still in my possession. He takes the keys and throws them onto a small hall table which is heaped with rubbish. Then he thanks me and gives me a sheepish grin which I'm certain would charm most people but no longer works on me. I follow him into the cluttered, dirty, sitting room and he makes space for me on the sofa so I may sit down. He offers me coffee, but I pointedly refuse.

"Is Belinda here?" I enquire.

"Um, yes, she is, but she's sleeping," he replies. "She had rather a late night last night and she's been a bit sick. I think she ate something that disagreed with her, but I'll wake her shortly to speak to you, if you'd like."

I'll bet she was sick, I think, but it was what she drank, not what she ate, that made her that way. I thank him and advise him that I'll interview him first and get to Belinda later. Then I open my note book and take out my pen.

"This all seems rather official," David says.

"I can assure you it is," I reply. "Death is a serious business. Now if we may begin. On the day of Steven's death, did you have cause to be in Rosa's apartment?"

"Yes," he replies. "She had a problem with the central heating and I went in to relight the pilot light."

"Is that all you did? You didn't touch any other part of the system?"

"I might have done but I don't really remember," he says vaguely. "I did ask Kurt to restart the heating if the pilot went out again, so perhaps he did something to it. I'm assuming there's some sort of problem with the system which caused the build up of carbon monoxide. I guess Kurt's death was a complete accident."

"I do believe his death was an accident but someone blocked the flue with a towel and I think that person was you, David. I'm sure you didn't mean to kill Kurt."

He stares at me blankly for a moment as if trying to judge how much I actually know and how much I'm guessing.

"As I said, I can't really remember what I did. Kurt, of course, had access to the heating, so it could have been him who messed up."

"Come, come, David, that's highly unlikely," I say. "Kurt used to work at installing central heating systems so he would know the affect blocking the flue would have. You, on the other hand, might not. I put it to you that you blocked the flue to stop the wind from constantly blowing out the pilot light and extinguishing the heating. I believe you had no knowledge of the danger your actions would cause and that Kurt was accidentally killed."

He considers what I've said but does not reply, so I continue. "I think it would be prudent now to wake Belinda. If you're not prepared to tell me the whole truth, I must question her about what she remembers of that day. She might be able to shed some light on things."

He's frowning and he looks troubled. He brushes his hair out of his eyes with his hand and exhales his bated breath with a hiss.

"If I tell you exactly what happened, do you still have to speak to Belinda?" he asks. "She's very upset about the whole rotten business and I'd rather she wasn't involved."

"That depends on what you have to say."

"You know Kurt's death was an accident, right. No one meant to kill him, or do any harm to Rosa for that matter," he adds.

"I would agree with that statement," I say.

"Very well, Danielle," he says. "It's as you say. I did stuff a towel in the flue to stop the pilot light from blowing out. I had no idea it would be dangerous and I'm devastated by what's happened. It was a complete accident."

He doesn't seem very devastated to me. In fact, he seems more interested in not disturbing Belinda's sleep than Kurt's death. Nevertheless, I can hardly contain my surprise that he has owned up to his actions. I get a jag of excitement because I know I've solved the case and I didn't expect it to be so easy to get a confession out of him.

"You understand, David, that I'll have to ask you to accompany me to my office so I can type up your statement and have you sign it in front of a witness," I say.

"Yes, I suppose that'll be okay," he replies. "Belinda will probably sleep for hours and I can pick up the car when I'm in town."

As he gets himself ready, I use my mobile to call the office in Ceret. I briefly explain what I'm doing and request that an officer meets me to witness the signing of the statement. They assure me someone will be sent over immediately. I practically have to pinch myself as we get into my car and head for town as I still can't believe he's admitted to the crime. I assume he simply doesn't understand the severity of his actions, but I'm not going to enlighten him until he's signed the statement.

When we arrive at the station, a young officer is waiting for us. He makes coffee as I type up David's statement then he witnesses the signing of it. Immediately after I have the document safely locked in my filing cabinet, I formally warn David and charge him with manslaughter.

"Manslaughter!" he cries. "What do you mean manslaughter? It was an accident, you said so yourself, Danielle. Why am I being charged?"

"I believe you didn't mean to kill Kurt, otherwise I'd be charging you with murder, not manslaughter. Surely you don't think a man's death can be ignored?"

He seems completely deflated and bewildered and I'm delighted as I really dislike this smug Englishman. I look forward to our day in court.

"This will kill Belinda," he says. "It'll push her completely over the edge. Do you understand what you're doing to us?" He jumps up and he is stamping about the room like a trapped animal.

"I assure you it's nothing personal," I reply. "I'm simply doing my job."

"Well fuck you, fucking jobsworth," he yells. "I suppose I'm free to go now."

"For the time being," I reply, unable to stop myself from smirking.

I show David to the door and he storms out. I'm really pleased that my colleague is with me because David's face was black with rage and I wouldn't like to have been here alone with him. He stays with me for half an hour while I sort out some papers just in case David returns then we both leave the office and I lock up. I decide to reward myself with a long lunch because I think I deserve it and I telephone Patricia from my mobile to bring her up to speed with what's happened and ask her to join me.

"My treat," I offer, "to celebrate my success." I'm delighted when she says she can manage.

The autopsy report from the doctor and the report from the pompiers should arrive in my office by the middle of next week and then I'll be in a position to send everything to Perpignan. This couldn't have happened at a better time, I think. Now if I can just complete the file on Steven's death, my promotion should be in the bag.

Chapter 36

I make my way round the corner to where the morning market is beginning to pack up for the day and head for the tapas bar. I arranged the time to meet up with Patricia but I'm very early. However, I don't mind waiting as it's a lovely day and it feels good to be out in the air.

To my surprise I see Alan and Charlotte at a table outside the bar. Alan is smoking a roll up cigarette and I presume that's the reason they're sitting outside. I haven't seen them since the day of Steven's funeral and I'm reminded of the conversation I had with Mark, when he told me some pretty scary things about Alan.

"Hello, Danielle, Bonjour," Alan says with surprise in his voice. "It's so nice to see you. How are you?" Alan stands and throws his arms round me. He embraces me like a long lost friend and plants a kiss on each of my cheeks.

"Danielle," Charlotte says slowly, stressing the 'elle.' "It's very nice to see you." She smiles benignly at me then she too stands and embraces me and kisses me.

"Please do join us. Will you have a drink?" Alan asks.

His speech is very slow and slightly slurred; he seems drowsy and not quite with it. I'm surprised because I've been told that neither he nor Charlotte drinks alcohol.

"I'm waiting for my friend so, if you don't mind, I'll sit with you until she arrives, then I'll have to move on as we don't have much time for lunch and there's something we wish to discuss."

"Of course, of course," Charlotte says. "We wouldn't dream of intruding. I'm going inside to fetch us some coffee. Would you like one?"

I decline the offer of coffee even though I do fancy one, as I don't want to feel beholden to them, but I sit down at the table beside Alan as Charlotte disappears inside. He rests his head on his hand and rubs his eyes.

"I'm sorry if I'm a bit off today, Danielle," he says, "but my medication has been adjusted recently and it takes my body time to get used to any changes. Charlotte helps me a lot with her healing hands and I'm so grateful for that, because before we met, life was hell for me."

"Why do you take medication?" I ask. "Are you ill?"

"Yes, and no," he says slowly. "I have a mental condition but the medication controls it. Some people shy away from discussing a problem like mine, but I think it's better to get things out in the open, don't you?"

"So Charlotte's treatments are as well as your medication, not instead of it," I say.

"Yes, of course," he replies, "I couldn't function without the drugs. I wouldn't like the person I'd turn into and neither would anyone else."

"Is that why neither of you drink alcohol. In case it affects the drugs you take?"

"Yes, that's right and we're much healthier without the booze. We used to enjoy a good drink but we don't miss it now; we've got used to not having it."

I am relieved that Mark has made a mistake about Alan's treatment and I feel happier knowing he is indeed on medication. The way Mark described him, I thought that, at any moment, I might have some kind of homicidal maniac to deal with and there has been quite enough drama in this town already. It also explains why he's sometimes slow to respond and why Charlotte is so protective and indulgent where he's concerned. As far as I'm aware, there are no outstanding warrants for Alan and the drugs he's taking should keep him sane, but I would like to know more about his condition all the same.

"Do you attend a doctor here in France or will you have to return to the UK from time to time?" I ask.

"I fell out with the UK doctors because they prescribed the wrong medication for me and I nearly died. If it hadn't been for Charlotte visiting me and taking an interest in me, I wouldn't be here speaking to you now. She realised I was becoming very ill and alerted the staff but it was touch and go for a while. I've transferred to Doctor Poullet and he's been great. His surgery is just around the corner, so it's very handy for me. He had my notes emailed to him from England within one week, which I thought was very quick and very impressive."

I have no reason to doubt he's telling me the truth, but I make a mental note to carry out my own enquiries with the doctor nevertheless, just to be on the safe side. I consider that, if they have chosen to leave the UK and come here for a new life, it's entirely their own business as long as it works for them and doesn't affect anybody else. Charlotte returns with their coffees and we begin to discuss their failed property purchase and the problem of recovering the money they paid to Steven.

"We've seen a lawyer," she begins. "And he's confident we'll get our deposit back eventually. He hired a forensic accountant who followed a paper trail that led him to our cash. Now our lawyer has frozen the money in Steven's bank account. He says there was never a bona fide legal contract and therefore Steven was simply holding the deposit on our behalf."

"That's very good news," I say.

"So it looks like we'll be able to afford to stay on here," Alan says. "I've found some work as a carpenter for a local building company and Charlotte has two clients for her healing hands business. It's all good news."

I agree with him then I notice Patricia walking across the square towards me, so I excuse myself and move to another table. When she reaches me, Patricia hugs me enthusiastically and tells me that she's very proud of me, and I have to admit, I'm pretty proud of myself too.

Chapter 37

When I awake on Saturday morning, I'm delighted to see the sky is clear and the weather is dry. Today is a carnival day and people have been working on floats and costumes for weeks. The highlight of the day is to be a parade and a party for the children of the town and the neighbouring villages. The parade will pass through the main street at two o'clock. The biggest celebrations will be on Fat Tuesday, Mardi Gras, which is next week. Then there will be even more floats and the entire town will have a day off work. Everyone except the essential services, of course, which includes me. Yesterday, two officers from Ceret arrived to assist me. We taped off parking bays in the main street and posted signs advising people that the street would be closed to traffic for most of the afternoon. They will be helping me today, once again.

I have always loved carnival days because, as a child, they were the special times when I didn't feel different from everyone else. It didn't matter if my clothes looked slightly odd as everyone else was dressed in fancy dress and they looked odd as well. All the children were treated equally when it came to receiving sweets or small gifts. My father and I always attended this carnival alone, when I was young, as my mother couldn't bear to take part without my brother. I still get the same feeling of belonging when I attend these special days that is sadly lacking for me during the rest of the year.

Patricia has the day off today as funerals are never held on carnival days. I'm meeting her in town for a drink when I get off duty at four o'clock. We can't get enough of each others' company at the moment as we want to discuss every detail about our prospective house purchase. For once, it's my colleagues from Ceret who'll cover the last shift and it is they who'll be responsible for taking down the posters, re-opening the parking bays and making sure the streets are cleaned for Sunday.

As I walk along the main street, I see many of the bars and restaurants have laid out tables and chairs along the pavement. People are setting out cakes, fizzy drinks and little gifts to give to passing children. Streamers and balloons line the route and some members of the band are already congregating to share a glass of red wine and to pass the time of day. One of the organisers of this year's carnival walks towards me. She's carrying a small package which she hands to me.

"This is for you, Danielle," she says, "It's a small thank you from the organising committee for all your work. We really appreciate being able to come here in the morning to a traffic free street; it makes our task so much easier."

I am overwhelmed as I have never before been given a gift simply for doing my job.

"It is just a small gift," she adds. "I do hope you're permitted to accept it. Just some pretty scented things that I thought a young woman would like."

I assure her I'm delighted to accept her kind gift and I find myself grinning like a fool because I'm so thrilled. I slip the package into my shoulder bag to open later then I make my way to where the officers from Ceret are standing. As there's nothing to do but hang around until the start of the celebrations, we decide to take the waiting turn about, so each of us will have one hour to sit in a bar or a café and relax. I'm to be given the first hour and I make my way to Claudette's bar where several of the locals have congregated. I order a coffee from Claudette, which she says is on the house, and I take the gift from my bag and open it at the bar. It contains soap, perfume and body lotion in a rose scented fragrance and everything is packaged with delicate pink ribbons.

"What a pretty gift," Claudette remarks. "It's not your birthday is it?"
I explain to her that it's a gift from the organisers of the carnival.

"That was very thoughtful of them," she says. "But it's about time they showed you their appreciation for all the work you do to prepare for these special days."

I've been doing the same work for years and, until today, I never realised that anyone noticed, let alone appreciated what I did. Perhaps, I've become more noticeable. I do feel as if I've changed. I feel more confident and more in control since the day Steven died. Maybe I just didn't push myself enough before. Maybe my superiors were right to pass me over for promotion because I simply wasn't ready for it.

When I think back to the sort of person I was just a short time ago, I'm amazed at the journey I've taken to reach this point. It's like an awakening and I feel that nothing can stop me now.

Chapter 38

The first of the floats comes into view and the oompah band strikes up with gusto. I'm standing at the edge of the street, about halfway along, and I can see that the first float is carrying around a dozen teenage girls dressed as cheerleaders. They are jumping up and shaking their pompoms with great enthusiasm and, although they are not quite in time with each other, they're being very well received.

I see many familiar faces in the crowd and it looks as if everyone is enjoying themselves. Although this parade, and the party that will be held after it, is mainly for children, there will be music and dancing in the streets for the adults well into the evening.

The second float holds the local under eighteens rugby team and a huge cheer goes up from the crowd as it passes by. Then a trailer carrying children dressed as animals comes into view and I can see Mark dancing along beside it. His flame coloured hair is flying as he swings his baby in his arms in time to the music.

"Hello, Danielle," he says as he comes level with me. "We're dancing and singing and shaking and moving, Daddy and Tom are laughing and grooving," he sings.

The baby is shrieking with laughter. Mark throws him into the air then catches him and Tom laughs so hard he begins to hiccup.

"Oops, I'd better slow down before he's sick," Mark says.

"I see you are well," I say, smiling.

"Mark and Tom are happy chappies. We're great, we are superb. Yes we are, yes we are," he says as he looks into the baby's eyes and pulls a funny face.

The baby shrieks and giggles and hiccups again and I can't help laughing at them because they are so comical.

"I've had good news, Danielle, really great news. The couple who wanted to buy the flat are back on board. I've just spoken to them, just within the last fifteen minutes, and they're back on board."

"That's wonderful news," I agree. "What changed their minds?"

"It seems their lawyer is quite confident they'll get their money back from Steven's estate and we negotiated a bit on the purchase price. They've both managed to get work, so they're less worried about how they'll pay for everyday things. They've always loved the apartment, so the deal is back on."

"That's terrific. Does Elizabeth know yet?"

"I've tried calling her mobile, but it just goes to the message service, so she's probably gabbing to someone. Tom and I are going to buy a bottle of champagne and a big bunch of flowers and then we're going home to celebrate with Mummy, aren't we Tommy, my boy?"

"I am so happy for you all," I say and I truly mean it.

"Yes, it's all good news and everyone is happy. With a bit of luck, we'll complete the deal within a couple of months, then Daddy, Mummy and Tom will all move to Spain before the psycho kills us. Yes we will," he says, and the baby giggles again.

"Oh, about that, Mark, I have some good news for you."

I tell him he was wrong about Alan and, actually, he is taking his medication. I also let Mark know that I contacted the British police and there are no outstanding warrants for him.

"Fantastic!" he exclaims. "That's fantastic news because I quite liked the guy. I just didn't want to end up as dog food. Now we can really celebrate."

He says goodbye to me, places the baby on his hip, then skips along the street singing "Tom Tom the piper's son caught a pig and away did run." It's an English song for children, I believe, and I sincerely hope he doesn't view Alan as the pig.

Most of the floats have gone by while we've been talking and everybody is having a good time. As the last of the stragglers make their way towards the hall where the children's party is to be held, I see Patricia waiting for me outside the café. There's half an hour to go until the end of my shift, but when I speak to my colleagues, they say they'll cover for me so that I may join my friend.

We make our way along the street and I tell her about my surprise gift and she's delighted for me. Then we stop at the pizza restaurant, which today is open all day because of the carnival. I'm feeling very hungry, so we each order a vegetarian pizza and a coke. Patricia takes her digital camera out of her bag and shows me the photographs she's taken from outside the little house.

"I walked up there earlier today," she explains. "I thought the views were spectacular and I wanted you to see them."

"You can't keep away from the place can you?"

"There's no problem, is there, Danielle?" she asks nervously. "You haven't gone off the idea have you? I don't want to push you into something you don't feel comfortable about."

I look at my friend as she stares at my face with her eyes full of hope and expectation and I realise that, over the years, she's become like a sister to me. Every event, every sad time, every happy time and every secret has been shared with her.

"My dear friend," I say. "This opportunity might just be the best thing that will ever happen to me."

"I love you, Danielle. You do know that don't you? Like a sister, of course," she adds with a smile. "I don't fancy you even though you are gorgeous."

I slap her arm and shake my head at her. "Idiot," I say. "Well, are you going to show me the rest of these photographs then?"

The pizzas arrive and we drizzle them with chilli oil and stuff our mouths with the delicious, hot food. There are artichoke hearts on the pizzas and they're my favourite vegetables because they're so light and succulent. When I bite into one, the juice dribbles down my chin.

"When we were children, we used to share one of these when your father brought us here for a treat," Patricia observes. "It doesn't seem so long ago does it?"

"Only over twenty years," I reply. "But we've done okay for ourselves; we've both got good jobs and, with a bit of luck, we'll soon have our own home. Now please stop being nostalgic and show me more of the photographs will you. We need to look forward, not back."

She wipes her hands on her napkin then clicks the camera and another picture comes onto the screen. It shows an amazing view down the mountainside and over the whole valley. Even though the weather is wintery and the days are still short, the mountain is very green because many of the trees retain their leaves. Every so often there are bright yellow patches of mimosa, and rich, burnished reds and golds of the hard wood trees. It's like a living patchwork quilt.

"That little house is going to be our home, Danielle, it feels so right. Everything is changing for us because we're no longer the frightened children of the school playground. We are strong, powerful women and together we can rule the world."

I stare at her for a moment. "Rule the world? I live with my parents and you live in a rented room. Let's be content to start with our own home, shall we?

"Well, tomorrow we can see about ruling the world, or perhaps the next day," she says and we fall about laughing at ourselves.

Chapter 39

Sunday, glorious, joyous Sunday and I'm not going to church, much to my mother's annoyance. Nothing is going to spoil this day. Not my mother's nagging, nor Father Francis's suggestions about possible suitors – Nothing. Instead, when my mother calls up the stairs to try to shame me into moving, I simply roll over in bed, bury my head under my pillow and go back to sleep, and I don't wake again until nearly lunchtime.

When I do eventually rise, I wash and dress then have breakfast, if you can call half a mug of coffee and two bites of a baguette breakfast. I'm excited about seeing the house today and also rather nervous because I want it to be perfect and common sense tells me it might not be. Patricia and I have been let down so often in our lives and I don't want that to happen this time.

I haven't yet told Patricia, but I've telephoned my head office and spoken with a very clever gentleman who is the financial advisor for union members. He went over mortgage figures and he very kindly explained the whole procedure to me. He assured me that I could easily get the level of mortgage we'd need to buy the house, even without taking Patricia's salary into the equation. I lied and told him Patricia and I were cousins and, under these circumstances, he's content to process a joint mortgage application. It seems that with my term of service, my level of salary and my solid banking history, the loan will automatically be granted.

I've arranged to meet Patricia at the municipal car park, on this side of the river, so we can travel to the house together. She suggested taking a picnic so we can discuss our business over a late lunch without being overheard. As the weather is fine, we plan to go to the picnic benches beside the bridge, but if it changes to rain, we'll just have to eat in the car. Patricia is bringing the food and I have a bottle of water and a bottle of wine. I had thought about bringing champagne, but champagne is for celebrations and I don't want to jump the gun and put a jinx on things. I look at the clock constantly and watch as the minutes tick slowly by, then I end up leaving too early because the wait is killing me. When I arrive at the car park, Patricia is already there.

"I knew you'd be early," she says. "I couldn't wait either."

She opens the back door of the car and places her basket of food on the seat, then she jumps into the front beside me. Before I begin to drive she plants a kiss on my cheek and squeezes my hand.

"Whatever the outcome today, we will move in together won't we, Danielle?" she asks.

"Definitely," I agree.

She sits beside me in the car wringing her hands in anticipation. It's a habit of hers that she's had since childhood, and I'm biting my lips, which is my habit when I am nervous. The drive takes less than ten minutes, so we arrive before the key holder, but it gives us the opportunity to walk around the outside of the house and get a proper look at the surrounding grounds. I regard my friend as she roams around the garden. Although it's very overgrown she still manages to recognise many of the plants growing there.

"We'll have soft fruits for jam making," she calls excitedly to me. "I've found strawberry plants and raspberry canes and, over by the trees, there are blackberries. I hope you like chestnuts, because three of trees are sweet chestnuts."

A car is coming along the road and we both turn to look in its direction. We're delighted when it pulls up and parks behind my car and a stocky middle-aged man climbs out.

"Mesdames," he says. "I am Monsieur Henri. You are here to view the house?"

We're a bit embarrassed to be caught looking round the garden but we greet Monsieur Henri and introduce ourselves.

"If you would be so kind as to wait outside for a moment, Mesdames, I will open the house for you to view. Please remember it has been closed up for some time so it might feel a bit cold and damp. It will take me a few minutes to open all the shutters; in the meantime, you may wish to continue inspecting the garden."

We are so excited we can hardly speak and we keep glancing at each other and grinning with nerves. He unlocks the front door, but before entering the house, he turns and says, "Did I mention that the walled garden across the road is also included in the sale? My father has a chicken coop there and the neighbour along the road has been tending the hens in return for the eggs. If you buy the house the chickens will be included in the sale, if you want them." He disappears inside to open the shutters.

"Chickens, Danielle, we'll have chickens," Patricia says clapping her hands with delight. "Let's go across and look at them while Monsieur Henri opens up the house. I didn't realise there was a garden behind the high wall, did you?"

Already in her mind, the house is ours, and I can't blame her as I feel the same way. We don't immediately see the entrance to the walled garden as it's round the side and partially obscured by some hedging. However, after a moment, I find it and we enter the large square plot of ground through a slatted wooden gate. The garden has several small sheds and a large chicken coop. We count eight hens poking about on the ground and picking up bits of grain before we are summoned back to the house by Monsieur Henri. With excitement and some trepidation, we enter through the front door.

"I'll leave you to wander around by yourselves, but if you have any questions, just call me. I'll be outside having a cigarette," he says.

As we step into the house, we realise it's not as we imagined it to be and, far from being a little house it is in fact rather large and surprisingly modern. Sunshine floods through the windows and the whole place is light and airy. The main room, which is at ground level, has a modern fitted kitchen situated to the back. There is ample storage space in this kitchen area and it also has a cooker, a fridge freezer, a washing machine and even a microwave oven. The cupboards are full of crockery, glassware, pots and pans. A comfortable sitting room is to the front of the house and the furniture, which consists of a dining table and chairs, a sofa and two armchairs, is slightly old-fashioned but very clean and comfortable looking. Although there are central heating radiators in both parts of the main room, there is also a large fireplace in the centre of the room and I immediately imagine Patricia and myself sitting in front of a roaring fire in the dead of winter, snug and comfortable in our own lovely home.

"I wonder if the price includes the contents," Patricia says, bringing me back to reality.

As we head up the stairs, we see there's a bathroom on the half landing and we're surprised to see a modern white suite with an over bath shower.

"This just keeps getting better and better; it's almost too good to be true," I say. "Are you sure you heard the price correctly?"

On the next floor, the bedrooms are situated side by side and each contains a wardrobe and chests of drawers that look as if they've been hand made about a hundred years ago. They are beautifully carved and have ornate handles. One bedroom has a double bed and the frame is contemporary with the rest of the furniture; the other bedroom has no bed so we assume that the elderly man took it with him to his son's house.

"The house is amazing," Patricia gasps. "I can't believe how fantastic it is. What do you think, Danielle?"

"I think that we confirm the price with Monsieur Henri and ask him if it includes the contents. If the price is as you thought, we'll shake hands with him immediately and tell him we'll have it, because it is amazing."

We head out of the house to find Monsieur Henri and he greets us at the garden gate. "Well, Mesdames, what do you think? Do you like the house?"

"Very much, Monsieur, very much indeed," replies Patricia. "We would just like to confirm some details please. The price, what's included in the sale, the entry date etcetera."

"Yes, of course," he replies. "Let's go back inside and sit at the dining table then I'll tell you all you wish to know."

He seems as excited as we are and I expect he's sensing that we want to buy.

When we are seated comfortably, he begins, "The price as discussed is 60,000 Euros and that includes the contents of the house, the walled garden and, of course, the chickens, if you want them. I'm looking to conclude the bargain quickly; the reports by the surveyor for lead, asbestos and termites have already been carried out and everything is in good order."

He pauses for a moment then says, "As you can imagine, Mesdames, everything has been maintained to a high standard because this is my family home and I wanted it to be comfortable for my parents. I have guarantees for all of the major work, such as the roof, the central heating and the windows. If you decide to buy the house, they will, of course, be transferred to you."

"Would you be so kind as to give us a couple of minutes alone, Monsieur Henri?" I ask trying to keep my voice calm and businesslike.

"But of course," he replies and he waves his cigarette packet at us. "I'll be outside," he says and walks through the open door into the garden.

"Oh my God, oh my God!" Patricia squeals and grabs my hands. "I want this house. You want it too, don't you, Danielle?"

"Of course I do. It's fantastic and we would only have to buy one complete bed and one mattress; everything else is already here," I reply.

"What do we do next?" she asks. "I have no experience of house buying. Do you know what to do next, Danielle?"

Thank goodness I'd spoken to the mortgage advisor because I do know exactly how to proceed.

"First, we'll shake hands on the deal," I say. "Then we agree on a notaire who'll draw up the 'compromis de vente' and we get to choose who we use for this. I'm going to propose Monsieur Buttonet because I don't know anyone else. When we sign the 'compromis de vente,' we'll have to pay ten percent of the purchase price as a deposit and we'll need to have that money in cleared funds. Do you have any money, Patricia?" I ask.

"Don't worry, Danielle, I have a good job and I spend almost nothing, so I actually have nearly eight thousand euros saved in my bank account. I've always been careful with money as I've no family to help or support me."

"I've got about the same amount," I say, "So it looks like we're ready to go ahead. We'd better tell Monsieur Henri."

We grasp each others hands across the table and give them a squeeze and Patricia asks me to do the talking because she's too nervous. When we go outside, we find Monsieur Henri leaning on the gate enjoying his cigarette in the sunshine. He's delighted when we tell him that we want to buy the house and he shakes our hands enthusiastically. It's arranged that I'll make an appointment with the notaire at his earliest convenience then telephone Monsieur Henri with the details. He's looking for the soonest possible entry date so that he doesn't have to keep travelling through from Carcassonne and that suits us as well.

After letting us have one more look around, he locks up the house and we say our goodbyes. Then we watch as he drives away. When he's out of sight, we grab each other's arms and dance around the garden like a couple of children.

"We'll have our picnic here in our garden," Patricia suggests and she lifts the basket of food from the back seat of my car.

We spread out our food and wine on the car rug that I keep in the boot and, as we sit in the sunshine, we raise our glasses and toast our new home. This is such a perfect day, I feel so happy and I know I'll remember it all my life.

Chapter 40

Today is Monday and I'm having the day off because tomorrow, which is my usual day off, is Mardi Gras and I'll have to work. I've come into the office so I can use the telephone in private to contact my financial advisor and the notaire. When I phone the notaire, he gives me a date next week to go and sign the 'compromis de vente' and I contact Monsieur Henri to tell him. He's very pleased that the sale is proceeding and says he'll come in to town and meet us at the arranged time. He also assures me that, once the notaire confirms everything is in order, he'll remove the 'for sale' board from outside of the house. He doesn't know the board has already been removed. I wasn't prepared to take any chances on someone else seeing the sign, so I took it down and laid it in the garden before Patricia and I left the house.

It's pleasant being in the office when it's closed. I've left the blinds drawn on the windows and door so nobody can see I'm in here. Although it's my day off and I don't have to work, I lift two files from the cabinet and open them on the desk in front of me. I've started my report on Kurt's death and it's just waiting for the autopsy and the pompier's findings to be added. There'll be no surprises as I've already identified the cause of death and the guilty party has admitted his crime and been formally charged.

I'm feeling powerful and successful and I get a warm surge in my chest just touching the paperwork. I truly believe the atmosphere in town has improved now both Steven and Kurt are gone. The Englishman stuck out like a sore thumb and many people hated him. Whenever I would enter a restaurant or bar where Steven was present, I could feel the discomfort he created. People were wary, they didn't trust him. He was out of place and it disturbed the normal order of things because he assumed his money made him better than everyone else. Now he's gone, his wife can take her money and her 'cousin' and leave this town. She can go back to where she came from. It doesn't matter how well she dresses or how much money she has, because to me, she'll always be a cheap whore.

As for Kurt, well what can I say? He was a despicable man and yet he had an easy death. Many people who are decent and kind have tortuous deaths but this revolting man simply passed away in his sleep. It doesn't seem fair, but life isn't fair. At least his death has restored some balance as Rosa is now back where she belongs. Her husband's sexuality should never have been an issue. He's a respectable man who's supporting her and their child. She should keep her mouth shut and stay in her place. If she wishes to act like a bitch on heat, she should be discreet and not bring shame to her family. Rosa is kind and is not disliked but she's a foreigner and she should be grateful for all she has. Many women would love to be in her position but will never have the opportunity.

I'm pleased that when David goes to court he may get jailed for his crime because that would remove another cancer from this town. Of course, there is always the possibility the Carter's will go under financially before then. Perhaps they'll return to England and I wonder, if that happens, whether their property might be purchased by Byron. This would remove another blot from the landscape. Byron is a good man and, given the opportunity, he would restore the building and once again make it a decent place for decent people to live. He and his family are here for the long term and he believes in giving something back. They are now part of this town and this community and I'm pleased because I like them.

Yes, the deaths of these two men have certainly improved things here and they've especially improved things for me. I'm now being considered for promotion and everyone is treating me with respect. They notice me when I'm working and indeed people who didn't know I existed before now greet me in the street.

When Patricia and I buy the house, we'll achieve another major step forward as neither of us will have to answer to anyone else. We'll be able to do whatever we like, whenever we like, in our own place. My mother and father can slip into the obscurity they've always desired because they'll no longer have to make excuses for my success.

I'm proud of myself; I'm becoming the successful, strong woman I always deserved to be and it's about time.

Chapter 41

Tuesday arrives and my mother is sitting at the table eating her breakfast when I come downstairs.

"Good morning, Mama," I say cheerfully. "Are you going into town today for the celebrations?"

"Perhaps I will. It depends on your father because I don't want to go alone and I know you're working. What are your hours today?"

"I finish at six but I don't start until ten so I'm meeting Patricia for a coffee first."

"You've been seeing a lot of Patricia lately, are you sure that's wise?"

I'm surprised by the question as Patricia has been my best friend since childhood and Mama has always liked her because she attends church regularly.

"Whatever do you mean, Mama?" I ask.

"My friends have been talking about you and Patricia. They say you've been seen dining together and embracing in the street. I don't think it's wise to be seen like that too often, considering you're no longer children and you're both single. I've been told Patricia is a bit different from other women because she's not attracted to men. People like to talk you know."

I'm deeply upset by what my mother has said. How dare she speak in such a derogatory way about my best friend and why has she not defended me to those poison mouthed hags she calls friends.

"We are doing nothing wrong," I say. "Our friendship is innocent, Mama."

"Your friend is not innocent, Danielle. She is guilty of a terrible sin. The church does not condone homosexuality; it's unnatural."

I'm beginning to get really annoyed. "Patricia's done nothing wrong. It's simply the dirty minds of your horrible friends, and I've done nothing wrong either, Mama. We've always been friends and we'll continue to be friends."

"Then I'm ashamed to say you too are guilty. You're guilty by association. You must promise me that she'll never again step foot in this house."

I am raging now. "Don't worry, Mama. I wouldn't expose my friend to such narrow minded bigotry."

She purses her lips and goes over to the sink to wash dishes and I know I'm being dismissed and the conversation is over. I had planned to broach the subject of my leaving and buying my own house. I've been worried about how my mother might react at the thought of losing not only me but my financial contribution as well. However, after this latest outburst, I decide to bide my time and choose my moment very carefully, as given what she's just said, I don't want to risk finding myself out on the street and homeless.

To tell you the truth, I've always been worried about what people might say about us. That's why it's taken so long for Patricia and me to make the decision about moving in together. In fact, if it wasn't for the discovery of the little house and its superb location, we might have kept putting it off indefinitely. I've spent my entire life apologising for myself and trying to please my mother. All I've ever wanted is her approval and I realise now that, even if I jump through hoops or turn cartwheels across the floor, I'll always be a disappointment to her. It's time for me to stop turning the other cheek when she hurts me. It's time for me to stop trying to make her happy because nothing I do or achieve will ever satisfy her.

It's with great sadness and with a heavy heart I leave my parents house and go to meet my friend. I've lived in this house for over thirty years and it's been familiar and comfortable in its way, but it has never been a home and I realise now that it never will be.

Chapter 42

When I meet Patricia, I'm still thinking about what my mother has said.

"You seem preoccupied. Is anything wrong?" she asks.

"It's my mother; she's upset me."

"Not again?" Patricia says.

"I think she hates me. I can never seem to make her happy."

"She doesn't think much of me, either, if that's any consolation," she replies.

"But I always thought she liked you. You go to church and she's mad about the church and everything connected to it. She never fails to let me know when she sees you there and then she scolds me for not attending."

Although I now know my mother's true feelings about my friend, I still find her bigotry difficult to admit.

"She tolerates me, nothing more. You know what it's like when people are polite to you then talk about you behind your back. Well, that's how your mother makes me feel."

"I am so sorry, Patricia. I had no idea."

"It doesn't matter. You're my friend, not your mother, and besides, it won't be a problem when we buy our own place."

"I just can't wait," I reply. "Now that all the arrangements are made with the notaire, we should be able to move into the house in under six weeks."

"Well then, no more glum face. Break into a smile, and your purse, and buy your friend a glass of white wine."

"Wine, at this time of the morning," I reply, with a look of mock horror on my face.

"I plan to start as I mean to go on," she says with a smile. "Today is a day for celebrations and I plan to celebrate with wine. Nothing and no one can bring me down because I'm so very, very happy."

I spend some time with my friend and arrange to meet her when I get off duty, then I go to join my colleagues. Several officers have arrived to assist me as there are a lot of people in town for the carnival. Many visitors have travelled a considerable distance to get here as this carnival is legendary. Throughout the day there will be parades, floats, fanfares and music, with much eating, drinking and dancing, including traditional sardanes. The shopkeepers spend weeks preparing for the carnival and there are many souvenirs on sale for people to buy. The sweet shop is particularly inviting with vividly coloured sugar-coated chocolates and bags of pink candy floss hanging on the wall behind the counter. The roads and pavements are already covered with a rainbow of confetti.

In the evening there will be a fancy dress ball and fireworks and all the townspeople will follow the symbolic carnival king through the streets for a 'Gregoire.' At eleven o'clock, people dressed as ghosts will follow the white-sheeted 'king' which is constructed from wicker. He'll be taken to the clearing beside the municipal car park and ceremoniously set alight.

My main role today is to ensure that the 'king' isn't tampered with. Several years ago, a group of young people from England bought a live rooster at the market and placed him inside the wicker king. They were drunk and mistakenly thought the celebrations had something to do with a classic film called *The Wicker Man*. If it were not for the vigilance of the torch bearers, who heard it squawking when they were about to light the fire, the poor creature would have met with a slow and terrible death.

The street is beginning to fill with people all jostling for a good position so they can watch the floats go by. There's a real party atmosphere and everyone is in the mood for fun. I spot my mother and father in the crowd but, after this morning's altercation, I pretend not to see them and just get on with my work. I cannot and will not take any more criticism from my mother today. And I hope my parents don't meet Patricia in the street, in case my mother says something nasty to her.

The owner of the café approaches me and very kindly offers to give all the police who are on duty the 'plat de jour' on the house. He asks me to give him a list of their names so his staff will know who to feed. I go and advise my colleagues and they're delighted. The two young officers, who I met when Kurt died, ask me to join them for the meal and I'm thrilled to be included and treated as one of them. It shows that, at last, they respect me as a fellow officer.

Chapter 43

I've been on my feet for several hours. It is now the afternoon and the celebrations are in full swing. I'm happy to report that, so far, we have had only one minor incident. A float, which was carrying several people dressed as trees, was travelling along the street. The 'trees' were carrying baskets of fruit with the intention of dropping apples and oranges into the hands of spectators as they passed them by. However, one over enthusiastic little boy lobbed his fruit at the crowd with deadly accuracy and managed to hit an unsuspecting man on the head with an apple. As the poor man fell to the ground in a heap, a massive cheer went up from the crowd who thought it was part of the show.

All in all, the day is developing into a great success and everyone is enjoying themselves. It's my turn to go for lunch and I join my fellow officers in the café, where we are very well catered for. A steaming pot of cassoulet and some warm fresh bread is placed in front of us and we all tuck into the delicious meaty stew. Many people come over to us to greet us and thank us for working on the holiday and, within a few minutes, a jug of red wine appears on the table courtesy of a fellow diner. Although we are technically on duty, we wash down our meals with the rich red nectar and none of us mentions it.

My colleagues discuss with me my handling of the incident at the Carter's apartment and praise me for keeping a cool head. They both agree that they'd be flabbergasted if my recent work didn't lead to a commendation or even a promotion as, in their words, 'the case is in the bag.'

After our meal we leave the restaurant. The parade is now over and the crowds are drifting away. Some people are going to watch the sardanes which are to be held in the market square whilst others are making their way to the outdoor theatre to watch a show. The street is still closed to traffic as there will be another procession tonight culminating in the burning of the ghostly king.

As we walk along the near empty road, I see a vehicle has driven along the street and has stopped at a crazy angle, partially blocking it. I begin to walk towards it to see what's going on. A man is sitting in the driver's seat, his hands are gripping the steering wheel and he's banging his head off the wheel. There's a beep, beep, beep as his head hits the horn over and over again. As I near the vehicle, I see the driver is David. He glances up, and when he sees me he pushes open the door and stumbles out. He's swaying slightly and his face is strained and angry.

"Do you know what you've done? Do you?" he yells at me.

I stop walking forward and my colleagues stand their ground just behind me.

"It's all your fault, you fucking bitch. Everything is your fault."

I'm not sure what to do about him because he's obviously very drunk, so I say nothing and wait to see what he does next.

"Belinda's in hospital. She cracked up when you charged me," his voice has raised alarmingly, almost to a scream. "I'm innocent. You know it was an accident, but you fucking charged me. She's had a complete breakdown."

I glance back to look at my colleagues and they smile at me nervously. A few of the people who were heading for the theatre are watching from the pavement, trying to decide which show they would rather see.

"And my children, my beautiful children." He holds his head in his hands and sobs.

"Has something happened to the children, David?" I ask. I'm worried that in his present state of mind he may have harmed them. "Where are the children, David?"

"Don't you know? And here was I thinking you knew everything," he replies sarcastically.

"You had to call them, didn't you? You had to interfere. You couldn't just leave well alone, you fucking busybody." He's ranting and spitting out his words.

"What are you talking about, David? Where are your children?"

"If only I knew. Social services won't tell me. You telephoned them, didn't you? And you told them Belinda was ill. So they came to my house. My house. And they found out from my Darling, from my Belinda, that I've been charged with manslaughter. She was so distraught that Social Services called a doctor and they sent her to a hospital. She's in hospital, all alone, with strangers. Then the bastards took my children away and they left me a note, a fucking note." He holds his hand over his forehead and sobs before continuing. "Now they've said I can't have my kids back and they've phoned Belinda's parents to come from England to fetch them. I hate her parents. Her mother's a bitch and her father's an interfering old fucker."

I glance back at my colleagues and once again they smile at me and nod their support.

David turns on them. "Are you laughing at me? Do you think this is funny?" he screams. "Is my family's tragedy amusing to you?"

"Please try to calm down, David," I say. "This kind of behaviour will only make matters worse."

There is a sizeable crowd gathering now and I know David will have to be removed.

"You stupid, stupid bitch," he screams, "It can't get any worse. I've lost everything. Everything. Don't you understand? I'm going to rip your fucking head off, you sanctimonious cow."

He starts to run towards me; the speed of his movement catches me unawares and I find myself struggling to prise his fingers from my throat. My colleagues waste no time in coming to my aid. Within a few seconds, they have his hands handcuffed behind his back and have placed him face down on the ground. Everyone is quite shaken by his outrageous behaviour.

"Would you like to read him his rights?" the younger policeman asks me his voice trembling. "The charges will be drunk and disorderly, breach of the peace, drink driving and assaulting a police officer. The stupid fucker broke the law in front of witnesses, so he's definitely going down for this," he adds.

David is read his rights and duly charged and the young policeman calls for a police car to remove him. I can't help feeling slightly sorry for David as he's dragged away screaming and kicking, but I know that if my colleagues hadn't come to my aid, I might have suffered actual bodily harm. So I guess he deserves all he gets. As for his children, they'll be better off back in England with their grandparents because both David and Belinda are completely out of control.

David's car is removed from the main road and the crowd that had gathered to watch the spectacle disperses and moves on. As my fellow officers laugh and joke with me about the incident, I realise I'm now being treated like everyone else and I've finally been accepted into the club.

Chapter 44

The autopsy report and the pompiers report on Kurt both arrive in the mail on Wednesday. I was expecting them to be heavy reading but I'm delighted to find they're very concise. It still takes me the best part of an hour to scan through them and familiarise myself with the contents. I'm pleased it's such an open and shut case and there are no complications. All that remains is for me to present my findings in the most professional way I can.

I'm wondering how best to complete my report. I want to present it in a detached and professional manner, as they would in *CSI* or *Law and Order*, but when I read what I've written, I sound more like the bumbling and inept Inspector Clousseau. I need Patricia with her report writing skills because this is very important to me, so I telephone her and ask for assistance.

"Of course I'll help you," she says. "Don't worry because I'm only working a half day today as there are no funerals booked. Why don't I buy us some sandwiches and come to your office at about two o'clock."

"Bless you, Patricia, you are a true friend," I reply.

"What's with the blessing?" she asks "Please don't go all religious on me, Danielle, or I'll think you're turning into your mother."

"Heaven forbid," I say.

"Oh dear, there you go again," she replies with a laugh.

When Patricia arrives, it takes her no time at all to prepare a very professional looking report and I get it ready to post to my head office.

We have our sandwiches and chat for a while, then she leaves to do some shopping because, she says, she needs to buy shoes before her toes come through the ones she's wearing. After she goes I open my file on Steven Gold and begin to compile a letter for Detective Gerard incorporating my comments and deductions.

I present my findings very carefully so the letter contains only the information I've selected. I want there to be no doubt about how he met his end and I want to be sure that I'm given the credit for closing the case. First and foremost is the evidence from various statements which show that Steven was not suicidal. I've included comments from Byron which tell of Steven's state of mind and disclose his financial position at the time of his death, to add strength to this opinion.

I produce a chart which shows the position of everyone who was in the building at the time he fell and selective statements to corroborate this. I believe this confirms that his death wasn't murder. It only remains for me to give an explanation of how he might have fallen, so an opinion of accidental death may be reached.

I can state with absolute certainty that Steven entered the building carrying his tool box and a 'for sale' sign because witness statements confirm this. When the balcony was inspected after his fall, it was noted that the sign was attached to the railing at the top and there was a string to attach it at the bottom, but this had not been secured. It was also noted that his toolbox was in the closed position and had been set down next to the balcony railing.

It does not take much imagination to place Steven on top of the tool-box, as he could have used it to give him height while he was leaning over the balcony rail to attach his sign. Anything might then have caused his fall. Perhaps something startled him, or perhaps he simply leaned too far over the railing and toppled. No one will know for sure what actually happened and Detective Gerard will accept anything I suggest and can prove, within reason, as he wants this case closed.

My report will say that, immediately prior to Steven's fall, I was in the street attending to an illegally parked car when I heard a loud crashing sound coming from the rear of the building, and the sound made me jump. It goes without saying that if it made me jump, then it may also have made Steven jump and, in this startled moment, fall to his death. It's believable and, more to the point, it's an acceptable solution to the question of how he fell. Steven's death will be deemed an accident. I'll be rewarded for closing the case and everyone will be relieved that the investigation is over. Most of what I say is true and, if there's the odd bend or twist to my version of events, will it really matter to anyone? I think not.

It is with much satisfaction that I send a copy of my work to Detective Gerard in Perpignan. I can now close my files on both of these cases.

Chapter 45

It's been several weeks since I sent my reports to Perpignan and there have been many good things happening to me and many changes in my life since then. The first was an email from Detective Gerard congratulating me for my exceptional detective work. As expected, he recommended me for promotion.

I was called to the city to sit an examination which, for me, was easy. I found the test simple and I achieved the highest ever recorded score. I've always been clever, even at primary school, so it came as no surprise to me. My mother didn't even acknowledge my success but my father telephoned me at my office to congratulate me. After that, the interview was simply a formality as Detective Gerard advised the board I not only had his full support but his respect as well. For once, it did me no harm to be a woman because times are changing and the police can no longer risk being seen to be sexist. That kind of discrimination is just not acceptable in our modern world.

The only downside to my promotion is that my office is no longer my exclusive domain. From time to time rookies are sent to assist me in order that they may benefit from my experience and training. It does, however, mean that on the occasional wet day, I may remain in the comfort of my office whilst the resident rookie goes outside to ticket cars and, on glorious sunny days, I'm free to take a walk by the river while they hold the fort inside the stifling glass box the office becomes.

Patricia and I completed the purchase of our house and moved in on a bright, sunny, April day. We've worked furiously on the garden since then and it's now ready for summer. The chickens are thriving in the walled garden and we now have four more as Patricia keeps 'rescuing' hens from the market. I've built some hutches and a run to house rabbits so we'll always have meat for the pot. Needless to say I'm the one who must kill and prepare them but it's a simple task that I carry out efficiently.

Our house is very comfortable and we've made very few changes. Now that we have our personal belongings installed here with us, it feels like home. Patricia has done wonders with her sewing machine and the soft furnishings and drapes she's made give the place a contemporary feel without taking away from the cosy atmosphere. We're very content here and it feels as if it's always been our home. Perhaps it's because nothing before did feel like home to us.

I see little of my parents now and my mother no longer speaks to Patricia in church. Neither of my parents has come to see our house, although both of them have been invited several times for dinner. I know my father has looked in from the street because I saw him one day as I was finishing my morning run. He must have taken a detour while driving to work. I called out to him, but I was too far away for him to hear me and he climbed into his van and drove off before I could reach him. I no longer beat myself up over my mother as I know now that the problems she has are hers and not mine. I still cannot understand her attitude towards me but I have other things in my life now and I can cope better with her rejection.

Neither Patricia nor I have thought about dating because we're not ready to share our lives or our home with any one else yet. We're enjoying finding our feet in this lovely house and I personally would be quite content if nothing ever changed. I'm really happy for the first time in my life and I want nothing to risk that happiness or complicate things.

I love it that when we come home to this house we can sit and dine together at our own dinner table. We can choose what we want to watch on the television or spend quiet hours reading in the sitting room. There's no pressure on us to behave in a certain way. We like nothing better than lolling about in comfortable old clothes and wearing our slippers, and if there are crumbs on the floor or dirty cups on the coffee table, too bad.

We're here in our home now and have just finished eating a superb meal that Patricia prepared. For the first time since we moved here, my friend is talking about the events which occurred all those weeks ago and changed my life.

She begins, "It's truly amazing that so much has changed in such a short time because of a ghastly event which happened quite by chance. It was so lucky you weren't immediately outside the building that day you heard the loud noise, or you might have witnessed Steven falling. It would've been a horrible thing to see. It was shocking enough that you discovered his body. I'm used to seeing death but you're not."

I stare at my friend for a moment and her innocent face is full of compassion. I feel she deserves a different truth from the previous one I told her.

It's very difficult for me to confess but I find the words and say, "Patricia you're the most important person in my life and I haven't told you the whole truth about what happened that day. I'd like to correct that now, if I may, and I hope you can forgive me."

I see a flash of fear and uncertainty in her eyes but she says nothing and waits patiently for me to begin.

"There was no crashing sound and I wasn't startled," I begin. "I was about to ticket an illegally parked car outside the Carter's apartment block when I realised that the car belonged to Steven Gold. When I looked up I saw him leaning over the balcony trying to attach a sign to the railings. Out of the goodness of my heart, I decided to give him the chance to move his car rather than just ticket it, because I realised he was probably expecting to be there for only a very short time. I climbed all the way up to the third floor to speak to him because the lift was out of service. When I called out to him from the entrance of the apartment, he didn't respond, so I walked into the room and onto the balcony. I was standing immediately behind him when I called out to him again, and it startled him."

My friend's hand is clasped over her mouth because she knows what's coming next and she's upset.

"It seemed to happen in slow motion," I continue. "He teetered for a split second and I reached out for him, but it was too late. My hand brushed his shirt but I couldn't grab him and I couldn't stop him from falling. Nobody saw me in the building. I immediately ran down the stairs and I was the first one to attend the body. I didn't want to be associated with his fall because I didn't want anything to jeopardise my prospects of promotion."

Her eyes are full of tears and they overspill and run slowly down her cheeks. She reaches across the table and takes my hands in hers.

"You poor, poor girl," she says, staring into my eyes. "What a terrible thing to happen to you. Why didn't you tell me about it before? Don't you know you can tell me anything?"

I'm surprised. She's sorry for me but shows no concern for Steven.

"You mustn't upset yourself over this," she continues. "It was a complete accident. It wasn't as if you pushed him, he simply fell. He was a horrible man, everyone hated him and no one misses him. You must put the incident out of your mind and we'll never speak of it again."

I couldn't have wished for a better outcome. I feel free now that I've unburdened myself and delivered this truth to my friend. I do as Patricia suggests and put the incident out of my mind. We leave the dishes in the sink and take a walk in the evening sunshine.

"We should plant a palm tree in our garden," Patricia suggests pointing to one that's growing on our neighbour's plot. "It always amazes me how resilient they are. They seem too exotic and fragile to be here in the Pyrenees, but somehow they survive."

Some do, I think to myself, but some fall over balcony railings and some are poisoned by carbon-monoxide. And all are incongruous and out of place and they always will be.

Chapter 46

ANOTHER TRUTH

To think that one simple act could change so much is amazing. I was the first one on the scene that day as I was about to ticket an illegally parked car outside the Carter's apartment block. I realised the car belonged to Steven Gold and, as I looked up, I could see him leaning over the balcony of the third floor apartment, trying to attach a 'for sale' sign to the railing.

I did not simply want to ticket the car, as it was parked in front of an entrance and might cause an obstruction, so I entered the building and headed for the lift. There was a sign on the lift, condemning it, as the maintenance contract hadn't been paid, but I guessed the power would still be on and it would actually be working. I didn't want to have to climb three flights of stairs, so I entered the lift and took it to the third floor. It moved silently, and fortunately no one saw or heard me. I've been able to confirm this from the statements of the people who were in the building at the time.

When I entered the apartment, I saw that Steven was balancing on his tool box and leaning over the balcony trying to secure the sign to the railing. He had the top fixed but he still had to attach another string to the bottom to stop the sign from flapping in the wind.

I called out to him. "Monsieur Gold," I said. "You must come down immediately and move your car. It's causing an obstruction." He didn't even acknowledge my presence. "Monsieur Gold, did you hear me?" I called again and I walked onto the balcony towards him.

It was then I realised he was listening to music and had earphones in his ears, but the music was so loud that even I could hear it. I tapped him lightly on the shoulder and he jumped with fright as he hadn't heard me approach.

He pulled off the earphones and snapped, "What the hell do you want?"

"You must come down and move your car," I repeated.

He was instantly annoyed. "Remove it to where exactly?" he asked. "Did you see any other parking spaces? That idiot David has sold them all and they're full."

"That's not my problem, Monsieur," I reply. "You must come down now."

"Or what?" he said scornfully. "What can you possibly do? Why don't you just fuck off? Why don't you just scuttle off under a rock with the other cockroaches?"

I've never been quick to temper, but something about the way he spoke to me and then turned back to what he was doing, dismissing me as if I were nothing, made me snap. In that split second, I pushed his shoulder hard and he started to topple over the balcony. For a moment it seemed as if he might manage to grab hold of the rail and save himself, but he was too surprised to make such a judgment. For a moment, I had the opportunity to catch hold of him before he fell, but I chose not to.

Instead, as he tumbled, I ran for the lift. I hoped and prayed I'd be able to leave the building without being seen or heard, and that was indeed the case. When I reached the ground floor, I quickly left through the main door and ran over to the body. I must admit, when I first saw him, I was more surprised than shocked by the way he had landed. Nobody had seen me and Madame Laurent, with her yapping dog, was confused and assumed that I'd simply run across from the pavement.

With jelly legs and shaking hands, I went through the ritual of checking for a pulse, being careful not to touch anything except his wrist as I didn't want his blood on my hands. The rest, as they say, is history.

However, please don't judge me too harshly, Messieurs et Mesdames, because given the right circumstances, we are all capable of murder.

Besides, I only kill people who deserve to die.

# # #

Dear reader,

We hope you enjoyed reading *Palm Trees in the Pyrenees*. Please take a moment to leave a review, even if it's a short one. Your opinion is important to us.

Discover more books by Elly Grant at
https://www.nextchapter.pub/authors/elly-grant

Want to know when one of our books is free or discounted? Join the newsletter at http://eepurl.com/bqqB3H

Best regards,
Elly Grant and the Next Chapter Team

The story continues in:

Grass Grows in the Pyrenees

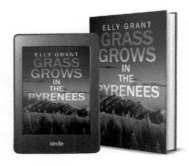

To read the first chapter for free, please head to:
https://www.nextchapter.pub/books/grass-grows-in-the-pyrenees

A Message from Danielle

Thank you for reading *Palm Trees in the Pyrenees*. I do hope you enjoyed it.

Perhaps you think you know me very well, but life is full of changes and I am at the beginning. If you would like to know more about me and the place where I live, then you may have the opportunity.

Also from Elly Grant, *Grass Grows in the Pyrenees, Red Light in the Pyrenees, Dead End in the Pyrenees* and *Deadly Degrees in the Pyrenees*.

Till soon
Danielle

Acknowledgement

For my husband for believing in me and for Pamela Duncan for giving me tough love.

About the Author

Hi, my name is Elly Grant and I like to kill people. I use a variety of methods. Some I drop from a great height, others I drown, but I've nothing against suffocation, poisoning or simply battering a person to death. As long as it grabs my reader's attention, I'm satisfied.

I've written several novels and short stories. My first novel, *Palm Trees in the Pyrenees* is set in a small town in France. It is published by Next Chapter. Next Chapter is now publishing the next four novels in the series, *Grass Grows in the Pyrenees*, *Red Light in the Pyrenees*, *Dead End in the Pyrenees* and *Deadly Degrees in the Pyrenees* as well as my other novels and a collaboration of short stories called *Twists and Turns*.

As I live in a small French town in the Eastern Pyrenees, I get inspiration from the way of life and the colourful characters I come across. I don't have to search very hard to find things to write about and living in the most prolific wine producing region in France makes the task so much more delightful.

When I first arrived in this region, I was lulled by the gentle pace of life, the friendliness of the people and the simple charm of the place. But dig below the surface and, like people and places the world over, the truth begins to emerge. Petty squabbles, prejudice, jealousy and greed are all there waiting to be discovered. Oh, and what joy in that discovery. So, as I sit in a café, or stroll by the riverside, or walk high into the mountains in the sunshine I greet everyone I meet with a smile and a 'Bonjour' and, being a friendly place, they return the greeting. I people watch as I sip my wine or when I go to buy my baguette. I discover quirkiness and quaintness around every corner. I try to imagine whether the subjects of my scrutiny are nice or nasty and, once I've decided, some of those unsuspecting people, a very select few, I kill.

Perhaps you will visit my town one day. Perhaps you will sit near me in a café or return my smile as I walk past you in the street. Perhaps you will hold my interest for a while, and maybe, just maybe, you will be my next victim. But don't concern yourself too much, because, at least for the time being, I always manage to confine my murderous ways to paper.

Read books from the Death in the Pyrenees series, enter my small French town and meet some of the people who live there — and die there.

To contact the author: ellygrant@authorway.net

Palm Trees in the Pyrenees
ISBN: 978-4-86752-921-8

Published by
Next Chapter
1-60-20 Minami-Otsuka
170-0005 Toshima-Ku, Tokyo
+818035793528
12th August 2021